FEAR OF DE SADE

FEAR OF DE SADE

Bernardo Carvalho

Translated from the Portuguese by
John Gledson

CANONGATE

First published in Great Britain in 2004 by
Canongate Books Ltd, 14 High Street,
Edinburgh EH1 1TE

Originally published in Brazil in 2000
by Companhia das Letras

10 9 8 7 6 5 4 3 2 1

British Library Cataloguing-in-Publication Data
A catalogue record for this book is available on
request from the British Library

ISBN 1 84195 496 9

Typeset in Van Dijck 12/18 pt by
Palimpsest Book Production Limited,
Polmont, Stirlingshire
Design by James Hutcheson
Printed and bound by
Nørhaven Paperback, Viborg, Denmark

www.canongate.net

For Henrique

ACT ONE

*T*here's not a chink of light anywhere. It's not surprising that the Baron of LaChafoi, with all his forty-
some years lived to the full, doesn't see anyone when he
opens his eyes. He doesn't understand why he's here. They've
thrown him into a stone cell — he could tell from touching
— and slammed the door. It all began a week before, when
he was awakened after a night of debauchery and excess,
surrounded by guards shouting insults and accusations. He
could hardly remember where he was — and nothing of
what had happened in the last few hours. Somebody had
been murdered but they didn't say who it was: 'Everyone
who is still alive is a suspect!' they shouted. As a provincial nobleman who had survived the Revolution, it wasn't
the first time he'd heard that. But since the upstart
Buonaparte had crowned himself Emperor, he had never
been humiliated in such a fashion. They were probably talking about the other three who had taken part in the orgy,

the baron concluded, without realising that, if there had been a murder, the most probable thing was that one of them was dead, and so there were only two left excluding him. That was what he underlined later to the tribunal – and it seems that it was that line of reasoning that determined what he later realised was his detention – insisting at the end that the last thing he remembered doing was swallowing the aphrodisiac in some aniseed pastilles. At no point on the agonising road which had led him in chains from the Château Lagrange, where he was found unconscious by the guards, to a local jail and to Bicêtre Prison in Paris, then on to the tribunal, and from there to the dark cell where he now found himself, did they bother to utter the victim's name; since they didn't reply to his questions, this explained why he had been taken for a madman for asking so many times who had died – 'as if he didn't know already' – that was what they retorted, in a sarcastic, reproving tone which did nothing to alleviate his ignorance. Since he'd been woken by the guards, he hadn't seen any of the other three, his fellow revellers, though he had already suspected, judging from his own fate, that since they were also suspects (at least the other two who must still be alive), they had probably ended up in the same place.

The situation was incomprehensible. Since they had woken him in the château — a ruin in point of fact, the only property left to him from all those taken by the Revolution and not returned under the Empire — until they had taken him to that dark cell, the baron not only didn't know the victim's identity and the details of the crime he was suspected of, but was ignorant of what people were saying around him. He didn't understand anything. They persisted in calling him by a name that wasn't his, although he never failed to point out that he had a noble title: 'Pierre de LaChafoi, baron'. This, in spite of the years passed under the Terror, when, under questioning from all kinds of authorities, he learned to renege all his aristocratic attributes, and collaborated willingly, thanks to the advice of his cousin, the Count of Suz, with everything the Revolution had demanded of him. Now, since he was really under suspicion, when he was woken by the guards he acted as if, after the years of the Terror, he had recovered his pride in his aristocratic origins — which would have been seen as suicidal fifteen years ago — and corrected them every time they addressed him in that strange language; just as later he had to correct the man in white who had taken him to the cell that to the touch seemed made of stone. After uselessly groping round it to find a way out, he must have fallen into a deep, despondent sleep, because when he opened his eyes again in the darkness in which he could see nothing, and said to himself, in yet another of his tautological reasonings, and trying to remember how he had got there, that this must be quite usual, since there was no light anywhere, a high-pitched voice welcomed him with a gloomy: 'At last!'

He wanted to believe that his eyes were still closed, and tried to open them again. As if they weren't properly open, he opened them wider, as wide as he could. He still couldn't see further than his nose. 'Who's there?' he exclaimed, backing against the wall from fear. But the voice only replied: 'If I were to tell you my name, you might not be able to bear the darkness, or my presence.'

BARON: Who are you?

VOICE: I prefer to spare you that.

BARON: What is this place?

VOICE: You must be joking.

BARON: No. Of course this isn't a prison, though it seems just like one to me. I should be free by now. They didn't prove anything. Where am I?

VOICE: There are other ways of punishing apart from prisons. Have you never heard of . . .

BARON: No! Not that! They've sent me to Charenton! How could they? Just because they had no proof. Is that the reason? Is that what they call a reason? The asylum was one of the possibilities put forward by the tribunal, but I told them I wasn't mad! I'm not mad!

VOICE: That's what they all say.

BARON: Charenton! It's not possible! But isn't it here that the Marquis de Sade is interned?

VOICE: Who?

BARON: De Sade! The marquis . . . That's it! Charenton! At least that's something. It's my last chance. Luck must be on my side in some way.

VOICE: That's the first time I've heard anything so stupid from someone who's just arrived.

BARON: The marquis will be my salvation.

VOICE: There is no salvation.

BARON: Do you know why I've ended up here? I'm accused of murder.

VOICE: It happens to lots of people.

BARON: Only I've killed no one.

VOICE: That's what they all say.

BARON: They don't believe me, but the truth is that I don't know who the murderer was – much less who died.

VOICE: It's no accident they sent you here. Prisons are for murderers. The asylum is for madmen. Each to his own.

BARON: I'm not joking. You may not know who he is, you might not even recognise him if you've seen him, but if this is Charenton, as you say . . .

VOICE: I've said nothing.

BARON: . . . he must be among us. And he's my salvation. I must find the marquis.

VOICE: If he's really the one you're looking for . . .

BARON: Years ago I heard that he puts on plays with the lunatics, that it's part of the revolutionary treatment. Have you seen any? You must have been present at one of them. It seems it calms the lunatics. Is that so? It seems that people come from Paris just to see them. Of course they're not going to let me meet him. They'll do everything to stop that. But I mustn't go crazy. Even in the worst moments, I've kept my head. I damn nearly lost it. I was saved at the last minute. Thanks to the Count of Suz. I'm not going to lose it now. I have to concentrate, concentrate. Who knows if the marquis might not be putting on one of those plays soon? If I'm in the audience, perhaps, when I recognise him on stage, I could have my say.

VOICE: Have your say?

BARON: I could get up and say what's happened to me.

VOICE: Why don't you tell the story now?

BARON: Only he can help me.

VOICE: No one can help you.

BARON: He could solve the riddle.

VOICE: What riddle?

BARON: The man's the devil himself, he's a genius.

VOICE: I've been here for a while and no one's called me a genius.

BARON: That's what he is. Tell me once and for all if you know how I can meet him. If you've seen him in the asylum. If there are any plays planned.

VOICE: Why don't you tell your story now?

BARON: Please!

VOICE: How can I solve the riddle if I don't know what it is? (*silence*)

BARON: Who are you?

VOICE: I tried to spare you, but since you insist . . .

BARON: Master?

VOICE: Master?

BARON: It's not possible! I must be dreaming. Tell me it's true! I can't believe my ears. What luck! Then it's true. You were chucked into this pigsty to be forgotten. After all you did for the Revolution. After everything you renounced. With me it was the same. They've not got the balls for the real Revolution. Now that you're old, at the end of your life, they want to do away with your name, silence your reputation. I always wanted to meet you!

VOICE: What are you talking about? And then you tell me you're not mad.

BARON: No, I'm not mad. See what happened to me for following in your footsteps.

VOICE: Let's start from the premise that everyone has responsibility for himself, all right?

BARON: (*enraptured*) Master!

VOICE: Don't call me master, you buffoon!

BARON: I can't believe my eyes. Pity I can't see you. You here, among us. Let me at least touch you.

VOICE: No! Don't do that!

BARON: At last, someone who speaks my language. Only you can explain to me what went wrong. We followed your instructions to the letter.

VOICE: Instructions?

BARON: The aniseed pastilles.

VOICE: I never gave instructions to anyone. What pastilles?

BARON: The ones from the night in Marseilles, with the Spanish fly, the aphrodisiac, remember?

VOICE: You're an idiot.

BARON: We did exactly the same thing! To tell the truth, it wasn't me. But the baroness swore it was the same recipe.

VOICE: That's all I needed! To share my room with a . . .

BARON: Baron, Baron of LaChafoi.

VOICE: Baron . . .

BARON: Only you can solve this mystery.

VOICE: What mystery?

BARON: Have you never heard of the night of Lagrange?

VOICE: What are you talking about?

BARON: From what I've been told, it was in all the important European papers.

VOICE: Once and for all, say what you've got to say.

BARON: I am a libertine.

VOICE: Ah!

BARON: Like you, master.

VOICE: Buffoon!

BARON: Stories about you go round all the most secret salons in France. I learnt everything from them. I'm a perfect disciple. I've heard them all, from what you did with poor Rose Keller on Easter Sunday (*he gives a shrill little laugh*) right up to the fascinating night in Marseilles. It's a legend already. And the baroness managed to get hold of the recipe.

VOICE: The baroness?

BARON: It was she who brought the crushed Spanish fly.

VOICE: Crushed?

BARON: According to the same formula you used.

VOICE: What formula?

BARON: The aphrodisiac, man! Sorry . . . sir. The aniseed pastilles! The baroness got hold of the same formula you gave to the four prostitutes on the celebrated night in Marseilles – she didn't tell me how. Don't pretend you're surprised! You're amongst friends. To my shock, she asked to be initiated, and planned the party along the lines of yours. She wanted to follow your night in Marseilles step by step. You, your vassal Latour and the four prostitutes. We had to adapt ourselves to the circumstances, since I was caught unawares, and instead of four women we had to make do with two. There was a girl as well as the baroness. For the first time, the baroness wanted to take part at all costs – her, of all people, minx!, she was dying to take part in an orgy after so many years refusing sex, so long as there were no prostitutes to make up the group, as when I'd organised my parties myself. There were only four of us: the baroness, my cousin the Count of Suz, who appeared with her at the last moment and also insisted on taking part for the first time: Martine, the loveliest maid the count could ever dream of having, and me. If my reasoning is correct, they must be here in Charenton too. They must have arrived this morning, like me, or not long ago. Yesterday, perhaps. Or maybe they'll be here tomorrow. If they're also suspected. You must have seen them. At least two of them. Those who survived. Whoever's not here is the dead one.

VOICE: The dead one?

BARON: The victim. It could equally be the baroness, or the count or even the lovely Martine, which would certainly be a terrible misfortune, an irreparable loss. I don't even know which would be the worst denouement for me. If it's the baroness, they might allege that I tried to get rid of her to marry the count's maid. Or that I wanted to get my revenge for her chaste behaviour during all these years, for the humiliation she submitted me to with her chaste wifely refusals, and that I decided to punish her during the orgy, now that she was finally submitting to my desires. Anyone who doesn't know the story, and doesn't know about everything she's put me through since we married, might think I went mad with jealousy when my own wife asked

me to take part in an orgy, after telling me she'd
been told about my debaucheries by my cousin, the
Count of Suz – the truth is, he bears no blame in
this matter at all, everything she found out about
me she heard in Marseilles and Bordeaux – and that
I decided to submit her to the worst punishments
so that no such temptation should ever again enter
her head. They might think I lost control and killed
her, a bit dizzy perhaps from the effect of the aphro-
disiacs – what a strange formula! – while she was
frightenedly asking me what was going on, what
these tortures were. They'll say that the punishments I inflicted on her got out of my control, and
that she finally died from the lashes I gave her.
According to the same hypothesis, they can say
that I killed the count for having revealed my nights
of debauchery to the baroness, but it wasn't him,
I've already said that. Or that I killed the count to
try and free Martine from his yoke. If Martine is
the victim, my love – but it can't be her! – they'll
surely say that I couldn't bear seeing her in the
hands of the count and the baroness all night long,
and that I killed her out of jealousy, and if I swear

once again that I was dreaming all the time – what a strange formula! – they'll say I'm lying. I don't remember anything. When I awoke in the morning, I found out that someone had died. Or rather, had been murdered. But I don't know who. Nor do I know who the murderer was. They arrested me on suspicion of murder. And the others too. I imagine so, because I've not seen them yet. I didn't see them when I woke up in the château. We're all under suspicion, waiting to be tried, I imagine. In court, I couldn't understand a thing. They were speaking a strange language. All those who were still alive are suspects, that's what I heard. If at least I knew if the others are here, who's here with me, I could find out who died. By process of elimination. Whoever's not here is dead.

VOICE: You're turning out to be a true son of the Enlightenment, my dear baron. If all those who survived are here, whoever's not here must be dead. That's logical. Apparently very logical. What's not at all logical is being accused of murder and not knowing who's been murdered. You have to be awake to enjoy the pleasure of murder, the greatest of all pleasures.

BARON: That's what I've said a thousand times over. I'm telling you I didn't kill anyone! I'm innocent! Or at least, as far as I know. I don't remember anything. The last thing I remember was swallowing the Spanish fly paste, your formula.

VOICE: I don't know what you're talking about, man.

BARON: I'm not accusing you, but the baroness assured me she'd followed your recipe. I spent the night unconscious. When I came round, the crime had already been committed, so they told me, and I was being arrested. They think I'm mad because I don't know who died, much less who did the killing. But they won't tell me, either. That's what my defence depends on! Can't you see? I have to find out who died to deduce the murderer's motives. Before they condemn me. Before they commit an injustice. Only you can help me uncover the crime, whose principal details are unknown to me. At least I'll be able to make them believe that it wasn't me if I can manage to explain what happened. But I don't even know that. That's what they're trying to prevent. They don't want me to know who died, because that way I won't be able to defend myself either.

VOICE: And what proves it wasn't you? That you're not lying? The fact that you don't remember doesn't mean much. Who can tell if you're not really mad, and committed the crime in a fit?

BARON: Master, I swear it!

VOICE: Don't call me master!

BARON: I beg of you. My defence depends on you helping me.

VOICE: How can my help be of any use to you? And why be so sure that I'm prepared to help you?

BARON: You're a man of the world. You've experienced many excesses. You've known women and men. Perhaps if I told you the whole story . . .

VOICE: Then what?

BARON: Well, perhaps together we could reach a solution.

VOICE: What? There is no solution!

BARON: A disinterested soul can see and interpret better.

VOICE: Who said I have a soul? And even if I had, why mine and not some other, any other?

BARON: Because you don't believe in feelings.

VOICE: What?

BARON: I'm not a proper libertine. I've got love and jealousy against me. Not like you. I'm a worm, a miserable slave to my feelings. I suffer from love and jealousy. Depending on who the victim is – and that's what I fear most – there'll be no lack of motives to incriminate me. But you, master, are the only one who won't take that into account. Your gaze is not only disinterested, but it ignores what they call the truth of feelings, which is no more than a great lie. You know that only the instincts tell the truth that hypocrites don't want to hear. You're the only one capable of reaching a right view of my story. You can ignore my feelings, which whatever they are have nothing to do with this crime, and unveil the real murderer, as well as giving me the arguments for my defence.

VOICE: And what, after all, is your story about?

BARON: My nuptials.

VOICE: You said it was a night of excess and debauchery.

BARON: Exactly. But for you to understand I have

to go back to the afternoon I got a letter from the
baroness, days after our first meeting, fifteen years
ago, when she led me to understand that she also
desired me and wanted to marry me, and prove
with me that God doesn't exist. Those were her
words. I like women who know how to use words.
It was the Count of Suz, my cousin and confidant,
who brought me the letter, days after that first meeting. In fact, it was he who introduced the baroness
to me, in what was left of his property. In the letter,
she announced that she was leaving the country
with her parents, emigrating to flee from the Terror.
Suddenly, just like that. Apparently, nothing of this
was planned when we were introduced to one
another days before. In the letter, she explained
nothing else. She only said she had to leave with
her family. She begged patience of me. And for the
sake of love I gave way. Out of despair, to see her
again at the end of seven interminable months, I
agreed to marry, which went against all my principles, and even against the Revolution; marrying a
repentant émigrée only made my already delicate
situation even more uncomfortable. At the end of

seven months' separation, I got a letter from her in which she agreed to return, to give way to my pleas and, at the risk of being taken for an emigrant, to suffer the punishment due to a traitor to the father-land – she knew how to use her imagination to excite me! – so long as she could marry me. She said she was ready for anything for the sake of love. She would come back in secret, if that was needful. I am a slave to my feelings, and it didn't take long for me to fall in love when the count introduced the baroness to me in what was left of his property. It only took a few hours. What a woman! When she disappeared into exile, my passion only grew. Passion makes one give way. I gave way again when, after fifteen years of marriage, she appeared, no more no less, in the château of Lagrange, in its ruins rather, the bit that was left when my other goods were confiscated, asking me for the first time to take part in one of the nights I had been organising in her absence. She spent the greater part of our fifteen years of marriage away from here. In Marseilles and Bordeaux, doing God knows what. Little did she know that this time, exceptionally, unlike all the other nights she had no doubt heard about in Marseilles and Bordeaux, there would be no orgy. I am a weak man. As I said, a slave to my feelings. And, with the baroness's travels, after fifteen years together, fifteen years of debauchery, given over to my instincts, fifteen years no different from my bachelor existence, I ended up falling under the spell of a girl. That night was to be the second time we met.

At this moment, terrified by what he thinks is a vision, the baron interrupts his story.

BARON: Forgive me, sir, I know it's dark, and I can't see further than my nose, but I had the impression I saw you for a moment. (*silence*) I know it's not possible, it can't be true, but . . . (*silence*) I had the impression that you are . . . black?
VOICE: As you've realised, it's dark. You must be hallucinating. It's common. The darkness produces visions, makes you see things. In the darkness, everyone sees what they want to see.
BARON: Of course, of course . . . Well, when my

cousin, the Count of Suz, introduced me to the
baroness, in what was left of his property, on the
eve of the Terror, I really was in need of a wife,
more because of the pressure of circumstances, to
save my own skin, since my fame was beginning to
make me an easy target for enemies parading as
revolutionaries. I was always reputed to be a libertine, marriage is against my principles, but the
circumstances demanded I got married, so the count
said. They never had the balls for the real
Revolution, master, and it was through trying to
follow its principles to the letter that I ended up
being forced to save my skin by marriage. Well, it
happened just at the right time, because she was
beautiful. And she wasn't getting any younger. She
had to get married. She managed to persuade me
after seven months' absence, although marrying a
repentant émigrée at that moment was riskier than
staying a bachelor, for someone with my reputation.
VOICE: If she was so beautiful, why hadn't she
married yet?
BARON: The count told me she was demanding. It
was thanks to him we got to know one another in

what was left of his property, and we married seven
months later, when I was already crazy, wanting to
see her again, imploring her to come back from
exile. She was very cunning. She was one of those
women who know how to hook a man. She knew I
was a libertine, and that I would steer clear of the
prison of marriage until the last moment, and she
knew how to conquer me. It was the perfect tactic.
After insinuating herself and seducing me, with her
little breasts tightly held in a silver corset, proposing that we should prove that God doesn't exist,
she disappeared for seven months, saying she had
emigrated. A shabby excuse. She can't have gone
anywhere, because, if she really had emigrated,
coming back would have demanded from her the
very courage whose lack had pushed her to go. It's
obvious. I'm not stupid. She accounted for it by her
passion for me. She said she would come back clan-
destinely. A shabby excuse. But a wonderful ploy
for seduction. I admire that. I admire women who
know how to use words and reach their objectives
with patience. If she really had left the country,
how would she not have problems in coming back

seven months later? Not even with the count's help, and his contacts, would she have been able to remain undetected. And all the letters she sent me? How did she manage that? She drove me crazy, begging her to come back immediately in secret letters which my cousin, the Count of Suz, managed to get to her, across frontiers and battle fronts, heaven knows how, and bringing me back her replies, minx!, spurring on my desire with the memory of her little breasts pressed into the silver corset I could no longer touch.

VOICE: Why did the count serve as intermediary?

BARON: Because he had contacts. He always had contacts. He's a man of the moment. First, in the National Assembly. Then under the Terror and the Consulate. And now in the Empire. That was how he managed to save what was left of his lands, and the ruins of my château. He knows how to tack with the winds. Hither and thither, hither and thither. The truth is, he was her accomplice. He wanted to see us married. And he knew me! And gave me his advice. He wanted to help me.

VOICE: Why didn't you go and see her where she was, if your desire was so great?

BARON: I couldn't. I would be taken for an emigrant, a traitor, can't you see? I would lose the château, the ruins left to me out of all my possessions. The guillotine would be waiting for me on my return. All the efforts I made to serve the Revolution, always under the guidance of the count, to save my skin and my château – the only thing I didn't give to the Revolution of my own will – everything would have gone down the tubes. They were difficult times, you know. Maybe I could have seen her in her hiding-place, if I'd known where that was. But she didn't tell me. Neither did the count. He said he couldn't, for his own safety and that of the baroness. And mine! He said it was for my own good; he was protecting me from my own passions. So that I didn't end up losing my head. It was part of her seduction tactics, no doubt about that. She wanted to be shrouded in mystery, minx! She couldn't leave France and then come back again without suffering the consequences. What a scheme! And there's nothing I admire more than someone who can cultivate someone else's desires. She knew how to make me lose my head. The letters were our only contact. And the things she said to me! How she described the heat of her body awaiting mine, which never came, never came, of course, because she escaped, she was my will-o'-the-wisp, my insatiable desire. That was how she conquered me. After seven months were up, when I could no longer bear it, when she was already pure fantasy, she wrote that she could only meet me again if we were to be married, out of fear of what I might do, of what I could do with her after so many months of pent-up desire. She said she might come back to France, minx!, putting her life at risk, if it was to marry me. And I gave in, for love. The second time I saw her was at the altar.

Again, the baron interrupts himself; he rubs his eyes.

BARON: Forgive me, sir, but I've just had that vision again. I thought I saw you. Are you sure . . . ?
VOICE: I've already said they're hallucinations. It's not surprising when there's not a chink of light anywhere. Go on with your story.
BARON: . . . When I saw her at the altar, there was

no going back. I saw that she wasn't the woman I'd imagined, of course. At the altar, they never are. And I knew. Marriage is one farce unmasking itself before another, in church, before God. After seven months of pure imagination, I had forgotten the reality I'd only seen once. But I was still blind. Only later, in the bedroom, could I see, in plain daylight, that I'd been betrayed by the cunning strategy she'd trapped me in, minx! The little breasts pressed into the silver corset were no longer there. She wasn't ugly. No, far from it. She was just a woman, like any other, and not the goddess I'd imagined for seven months. More than anything, because she wanted nothing to do with me. She acted the role of wife unconvincingly, and whenever she could she kept clear of me. The marriage was never consummated. Quite to the contrary of what she wrote during those seven months of absence in her letters inflamed with desire, now all she wanted to do was keep her distance. It was as if suddenly she'd turned around, changed her mind. But that only drove me crazier. I was ready to do anything, to rape her if necessary, if she went on with this act.

But before I had the chance, a week after the
marriage, she had already gone back to Marseilles,
sorting out family matters, as always. She knew how
to bargain. She spent all her time keeping her
accounts. She calculated everything. And that is
what she did with me. She tricked me. The differ-
ence was that now she no longer needed to write
letters. She was tied to me by marriage. She'd got
what she wanted. She didn't need to keep the flame
of desire alive. During the fifteen years of marriage,
we spent most of the time apart. You can't take
anything with you from this world, so make the
most of it, and that's what I've done. Straightaway
I saw the convenience of the situation, and what
she was proposing to me in her silent self-removal:
proving that God doesn't exist. I was to go on with
my libertine existence and leave her in peace, and
in exchange I'd have all the alibis of marriage, as
would she. It was a kind of contract. She knew
how to strike a deal. She got what she wanted. She
was getting on. She needed to get married. The
parties in the Lagrange château, what was left to
me of the ruins, became famous, while the baroness

spent her life in the city, taken up by her duties and business affairs, without bothering me. At least that was what she said, although more than once she was seen in Marseilles and Bordeaux, in elegant receptions and dinners, in the company of those people who are still having a good time in spite of the country's collapse. They were fifteen years of a tacit agreement which was very convenient to me. Until I met Martine, the maid the Count of Suz couldn't even dream about. The girl I told you about. I planned the Lagrange night only for her.

VOICE: And the count?

BARON: He appeared that night too, but only at the last moment.

VOICE: No, you numbskull! In those fifteen years! What happened to him in those fifteen years, after the Terror?

BARON: He was my greatest confidant. He was often at my side. I owe him my life. He's a man of the world, with many contacts. More than once he managed to stop my name being included in lists of suspects. He never took part in an orgy at the château, but he got me the men and women I needed.

He never wanted to take part. And it wasn't for
lack of invitations. I wanted to pay him back for so
many favours, but he always declined my offers. It
just seems that my nights weren't to his taste. Until
the last one, at least. For on this last occasion, it
was he who invited himself. At the last moment.
And I accepted, of course. I couldn't refuse. He had
my best interests at heart. He understood my
philosophy. And he respected me. As soon as the
baroness started with her stories and went away to
Marseilles, he procured the best women in the
region for me. Once, he even brought three prostitutes from Paris. He got the prettiest women in
the Midi, who were up for anything. He helped me
to understand the baroness's caprices, that she
wasn't a woman for the bedroom, and made me
understand that she had her own reasons. He had
his own little domestic problems. The countess, so
it seems, also spent most of her time away from
the count. She hated provincial life. That was what
she said. And my cousin led me to understand that
certain women don't appreciate the pleasures of the
flesh. Because their instincts have been undermined

by convention. How on earth did I believe him? It's true that it was a great consolation to know that he had gone through the same humiliation that I was suffering now, but that idea that the baroness, like the countess, might have had her instincts undermined, only strengthened my will to corrupt her and debase her to bring them to the surface. He hardly saw the countess. They had no children. He must have consoled himself in some other way. But I didn't ask. The count is a discreet man. I owe him the discretion with which he brought his consignments of women and men to the château, the most depraved examples of the species, risking himself even under the Terror. Just as he helped me, he must have got his own benefits from these contacts. It's strange that you've never heard of the Lagrange nights, and in particular of the last, which was in all the important European papers from what they tell me, although it didn't even come close to the previous ones for debauchery. There were only four of us. I was taken by surprise. It wasn't intended to be an orgy. It was a special night for the count's maid. It's true that no one had died on the other occasions, but nothing was planned, believe me. Unlike the others, which I planned in every detail, often with the count's collaboration, I didn't expect guests for that night. I had to change the plans at the last moment, because of the baroness. It was completely unexpected and out of order. I'd planned a night alone with Martine, the count's maid; I met her just when I'd decided to look for him in what was left of his lands, something I'd not done since I'd known the baroness, fifteen years earlier. Since that lunch in which he introduced the baroness to me, he'd always procured the women and the men I needed. And since meeting the baroness, I'd never returned to what was left of the count's lands. He was always very obliging. It was he who came to see me. He took the initiative before I even thought about going over to see him. But now it was more than a month since he'd last appeared. More than a month with no news of him, and I needed more individuals willing to take part in a night I'd been imagining for some time. The count might be ill, or even have died in a duel or, worse, have been included in the list of traitors, under false accusation of one of the Emperor's toadies. Someone with so many contacts attracts many enemies too, and this world is full of slanderers. He'd always been so helpful, and the least I could do was to go and look for him in what was left of his property, and go to his aid if it should be necessary. That was when the miracle happened. When I least expected it. There she was, this thing of beauty. It's curious that, fifteen years after the baroness, I should have met Martine, both of them in what was left of the count's property. And that I should have fallen in love with both. When I arrived at what was left of the count's property, neither he nor the countess were there. I feared the worst. He was a clever man. At the worst moments, he had to let part of the property and his possessions go to keep the best part. He understood the situation. He managed to keep in with the right people. And he gave me advice. But one never knows. With so many interests involved, his allies might be the first to stab him in the back. From what they told me, the countess hadn't set foot there for years. And they told me nothing of the count. Only that he wasn't there. That was when

the miracle happened. She appeared from the back
of the house, she was a wonderful girl, with her
breasts pressed into the silver corset like the ones
I still had the memory of from the first time I saw
the baroness, the same little breasts, covered by the
golden hair falling over her shoulders. Where had
this creature come from? Was she the last maid left
to the count? She was the baroness as I had imagined her the first time and all through the seven
months I didn't see her before our marriage. She
was a mirage. The most beautiful woman. The
baroness as I had imagined her during seven months
of waiting, and who had disappeared when I saw
her at the altar and, above all, with her refusal to
give in to my growing desires to debase her. I asked
her name and she told me. I asked how old she was
and she told me. Fifteen. She also said that the
count would only be back the following week. He'd
gone to Paris. I asked how long she'd been there.
She laughed. She said: Forever. That explained it.
I hadn't been in what was left of the count's lands
for fifteen years. So I couldn't have seen her. Then,
she whispered to me that, in fact, she had fled from

a convent where she was being prepared to be a
novice. Before the mother superior could use her,
which was more than understandable. And she'd
ended up there as a servant. Straight away, I invited
her to visit me. I could feel a thirst for vengeance
in her eyes, though I couldn't think what for. She
had fine skin and hands. It's quite usual for a girl
like her to rebel against her condition. And the fact
that I might be of use to her to take her revenge
on the world only excited my senses the more. My
body at the service of a maid's vengeance. She
smiled, with her full lips. I tried to kiss them, but
she drew back. She feigned timidity. She was for
me: treacherous in her purity. I did everything to
persuade her to come and see me in the château.
I didn't tell her it was nothing more than a ruin. I
promised to get her out of there and she began to
laugh, laugh a lot, so much that she scared me. I
thought I might have sent her mad. But she soon
pulled herself together. She knew what she was
doing, and that's something I admire. I admire women
who know how to seduce and to use words. She was
for me. I forgot my orgies. I forgot everything else

I'd gone there to do. It was her I wanted. I asked
her to come to the château of Lagrange before the
count came back, on the night of the second
Saturday in the month, when I planned my orgies.
But this time, I explained, it would be a night for
her alone. I was in love. I fall in love very easily. I'm
not a proper libertine; I'm a slave of my instincts
but of my feelings too. She smiled and accepted.
With a great deal of reluctance. She said she would
come on Saturday before the count came back. I'll
send someone to bring you, I said. I saw she was
delighted. I saw her breathing nervously, panting
inside her corset. She was mine. Please understand
that for her I was not planning an orgy. It was, exceptionally, a night only for two. That's why I couldn't
believe my eyes when the count appeared at château
Lagrange, well before his planned return, exactly
on the night of the second Saturday in the month,
when I usually laid on my orgies, and on top of that
bringing the baroness, whom I'd not seen for
months. They appeared a few hours before the maid.
I couldn't believe what I heard and saw. For the first
time in fifteen years, the baroness was asking me if

she could take part in one of the nights in the
château. The baroness, my wife. She said she'd heard
stories of my fame in Marseilles and Bordeaux. After
fifteen years, she was ready to discover the pleasures of sex. I burst out laughing. But the count
didn't laugh, and nor did she. I laughed out loud.
What an irony! After so many years dreaming of
deflowering her. Just at this moment, when I'd found
this light on my path. It was all very inconvenient.
I pulled the count over into a corner. I asked him
to help me once more and take the baroness away;
she was spoiling my night. He said he thought it
better for me to agree with what she was asking of
me. He said he would take part too, out of soli-
darity with me. With me? I shouted, and started
laughing again. That was when he asked where the
maid was. I don't know how he'd found out.
Probably one of the other servants who worked on
the land or in the stables, or some witch tired of
cleaning up cowshit and envious of Martine's
beauty, had betrayed her. I answered, trying to hide
my surprise, that she ought to arrive at any moment,
I'd sent a carriage to fetch her, and asked him where

he'd found such a beautiful creature. As I asked him
I laughed, but he didn't. Nor did he reply. Before
I'd pulled him over into the corner, the baroness
had told me that she'd got hold of the formula for
your aphrodisiac, master, the Spanish fly one. She
was anxious as she spoke, nervous, and ready to
enjoy the party. It would be just now, when I was
in love with someone else, after fifteen years
of debauchery trying to forget her, fifteen years of
absence, that she wanted to take part in one of my
orgies. And the count! I tried to tell him I was in
love, and that I'd even thought, exceptionally, of
not laying on an orgy that Saturday. I had to speak
carefully so as not to offend him, now that he too
said he was ready to take part, an eleventh-hour
sodomite. But he repeated that he didn't think it
was a good idea to disappoint the baroness. The
count and I saw eye to eye. I decided to accept his
advice. My meeting with Martine would be put off
to another occasion. Immediately after talking about
the Spanish fly, the baroness said that she had only
one demand, since it was the first time: beyond the
count and me, she only wanted one other woman,

and we should not get a prostitute for her. Little
did she know that that night I was only expecting
the count's maid and no one else. I had no orgy
prepared. Only the fifteen-year-old maid, ready to
be deflowered. Just like with the baroness, when I
saw her for the first time in what was left of the
count's property, it had been a blinding flash, what
the hypocrites call love at first sight. I wasn't going
to let the two of them spoil everything. If at least
I could prevent Martine arriving and substitute her
for a prostitute, I would satiate the baroness's inconvenient desires on that Saturday, and the following
one bring the maid back again. But the baroness
would not have a prostitute on her first night of
debauch. I racked my brains. I couldn't lose everything because of the caprices of a minx who for
fifteen years repelled all my advances, rightful as
they were. What did she want now, with her sudden
conversion to sex? That was what I asked the count,
irritated as I was by having to change my plans.
And he replied that women can smell things a long
way off. They have a sixth sense. Just now, when I
was in love with another, she asked me to be

subjected to punishment from my whip. She wanted to be corrected by her husband, to be punished for her fifteen years of dereliction of duty, and she was even providing me with the aphrodisiac. At the same time as I felt frustrated of my night of love – I had decided to keep to my encounter with Martine, I wanted to discover alone the perfidiousness of those fifteen years of purity – I confess I couldn't contain my excitement at the prospect of soon beating the baroness, that minx!, after fifteen years of respecting her chaste refusals. She was no longer the woman I had known in what was left of the count's property. Nor even the one I had met again at the altar seven months later. I tried to make the count convince her that none of this made the least sense. Useless. My only solution was to wait. The baroness said: a chamber orgy. It was plain she didn't know what she was talking about. Whoever's heard of that! A chamber orgy! The baroness! She said: I want to be initiated with a discreet ceremony. As if she was talking about a late christening. I confess it passed through my brain that my hour of revenge had come after fifteen years of prudish rejection, the mare! I imagined subjecting her to the horrors of a libertine night, and debasing her to the point of death. She fully deserved it. But it was only a thought, interrupted by the sight of the count entering what was left of the château salons with my sweet Martine. He'd gone to wait for her at what was left of the gateway. They really had decided to put paid to my happiness. The baroness had put a platter on the table with the aniseed pastilles in which she'd dissolved the Spanish fly paste according to the formula she'd got hold of. On the journey, which had taken two days, from Bordeaux to Lagrange, she'd gone by an alchemist's, and he'd made her the paste according to the formula she'd got hold of, heaven knows how. She got to the château exhausted by the journey. She said: I have to retire to my apartments. She disappeared while the count was waiting outside for his maid. And she only came back when the count came back in; he came into the château, followed by the maid. Martine had the countess's clothes on. It was as I'd thought. She didn't think she'd be caught *in flagrante*. She must have tried the countess's clothes on when

the count wasn't there. She was still more beautiful. But now, instead of the proud expression of
someone prepared to avenge herself on the world,
which I'd had a glimpse of and which had excited
me so much in what was left of the count's property, her eyes were lowered, and she had a submis-
sive, fearful attitude, like a slave. She said nothing.
Not even when I spoke to her, welcoming her and
asking if she'd had a good journey. Of course that
wasn't the way I wanted to receive her. But I
preferred to explain nothing in front of the count
and the baroness. The whole situation had become
very inconvenient and embarrassing. All I wanted
to do was take Martine into a corner, explain the
misunderstanding and kiss her little breasts. I had
to deflower her one way or another, before they did
it, so that she'd never forget me. But when it wasn't
the count that wouldn't leave me alone with her, it
was the baroness. The wine was already on the table,
next to the aniseed pastilles, but she didn't touch a
drop. I asked if she wasn't thirsty. She didn't answer.
It was too late. The baroness offered us the pastilles.
And the last thing I can remember is eating them.

VOICE: They brought a couple in yesterday morning.

BARON: What do you mean?

VOICE: Yesterday morning, a day before you, they brought a couple in.

BARON: A couple?

VOICE: I saw them both in the refectory.

BARON: Where is it?

VOICE: It's no use. You can't go there. You can't go out of here.

BARON: But you went there. Wait a bit (*he rubs his eyes*), I think I can see things again. Are you certain that . . . ?

VOICE: That's enough! It's dark. You're nervous. You'll end up seeing what you want to see. Do you want me to help or don't you?

BARON: What were they like? Eh? Did he have a goatee? Did she have fiery red hair?

VOICE: The description fits like a glove.

BARON: (*horrified*) Then it's them?

VOICE: Maybe.

BARON: And wasn't there a beautiful girl with them, about fifteen, with her breasts pressed into a silver corset and with golden hair falling over her shoulders? Wasn't there?

VOICE: No. I'm sorry, but I didn't see anyone fitting that description.

BARON: (*covering his face with his hands*) It's not possible! There's no justice in the world! Then it's her! My God!

VOICE: Careful! Religion is caused by laziness and impatience. It's the great defect of anyone who tries to explain the inexplicable without using reason. Don't reach hasty conclusions.

BARON: But it's her! It's her!

VOICE: (*impatient*) Her? Who?

BARON: She's the dead one. They killed her! While I was asleep!

VOICE: I wouldn't go that far. What makes you so sure?

BARON: Murderers!

VOICE: I heard the two of them talking in the refectory. They said they wouldn't stay for long. They think they'll be found innocent. Idiots.

BARON: I need to see them.

VOICE: It's impossible You've no access to them.

They're under observation. You can't go back there.

BARON: Why not?

VOICE: This is where the definitive ones stay.

BARON: Definitive?

VOICE: Those who've come to stay.

BARON: But you're here and you went there.

VOICE: I have free passage. I've been here for some time. It's a right you achieve with time.

BARON: And what did they say? What did they say?

VOICE: They'd just got here. They were huddled together, frightened to mix, which only excited the others more – they surrounded them as if they were about to jump on them, and then ran around laughing all over the place. It was difficult to come near them without their hair standing on end. It was only at lunchtime, while all of them were eating, that I could get close without them realising it, and hear what they were saying. They were whispering, like people planning an escape. I couldn't help getting interested. Attempts to escape interest me. Even if it's only because of the punishments those who try are subjected to. But they weren't planning any escape. They thought they would be

released soon. They were saying that there was no
reason for the two of them to be kept here. No one
could prove anything against them. The man, who
was in a deplorable state, dishevelled and dirty, was
trying to calm her down, saying that they'd soon
be free. He said they weren't mad. That's what they
all say. They said they'd been sent here for lack of
proof, on the excuse that they'd lost their reason,
until the court found something to incriminate them
with. They would soon be freed. He said they had
contacts. That confirms your story. She said over
and over: 'What a nightmare! What a nightmare!',
shaking her head and with her eyes glazed over as
if she were mad and had come to the right place.
He did everything to comfort her. But there was
also something mad in what he was saying: 'Some
things are inevitable. It was better this way. God works
in mysterious ways,' and other such idiocies. God! It's
the first name that comes into their mouths when
things get difficult, but they never think of Him when
they loosen the reins of pleasure, like unbelievers.
They enjoy themselves without thanking anyone, and
only remember God when they get into trouble.

And that's when they go mad, when they realise that God doesn't exist and never did, at the moment they most need Him, when they've given their lives as proof that He doesn't exist. Poor hypocrites. It was only little by little that I was able to observe the nods of the head and the gestures with his arms he punctuated his soothing speech with; those tics became more and more bizarre. If I was a doctor, after what I've seen in this place, I wouldn't discharge them. Not a bit of it. Simply observing them, they seemed really mad to me.

BARON: They're not mad. It might not be them.

VOICE: Unfortunately, I think it is them. They were talking about a night in the château and about the victim . . .

BARON: Martine!

VOICE: . . . as someone they knew closely.

BARON: They were in league!

VOICE: Something might have gone wrong. The woman simply repeated: 'What a nightmare! What a nightmare!', with the same movement of her head and glazed eyes. She was very low, her face looked exhausted. And he said to her: 'Now, she's gone.

She's a long way off. There's nothing more we can do. We have to accept facts and destiny.'

BARON: Murderers! That's the confession the court needed to arrest them. The proof of my innocence!

VOICE: It's a long way from there to make them confess anything to the representatives of justice. Though it's not a bad idea. Forced confessions are often the most beautiful ones, the ones that expose the tragic, powerless destiny of man, all the falsity of justice and the illusion of liberty and free will.

BARON: Someone has to make them pay for the crime they committed.

VOICE: They don't seem so worried about that. They think they're going to get out soon. Now, thinking about you, I don't know who's more naïve, you or them. Pay! Nobody pays for anything and everyone pays for everything. Life is an incentive to crime. What kind of a libertine are you?

BARON: Not a proper one, I told you. A slave to my feelings.

VOICE: That's why you're blind. You can't see a thing.

BARON: There's not a chink of light anywhere.

VOICE: It's one of the features of this wing. In the

other wing, at least they can see one another. Or they think they do. Which doesn't reduce the madness in the least. Maybe it just increases it. Sometimes, it's worse to be able to see. There's no use in seeing when everything around you is a hallucination. I'm not excluding the possibility that your companions at the orgy might be hallucinating too when they think they're going to get out soon. They're just as mad as the others. Maybe even more so. How come they think they're going to be released?

BARON: If I was incriminated instead of them.

VOICE: No one escapes the latest medicine. They're under observation. If I was a doctor, I'd never let them out again. Look at his tics while he was trying to comfort her and the way she shook her head, backwards and forwards, while she listened and repeated 'What a nightmare! What a nightmare!' Leave it to the doctors, they know what they're doing. They're the worst executioners. I doubt your friends will ever return to the world of reason. I say so myself, and I've been through a lot.

BARON: But someone has to pay for the crime.

VOICE: What teachings did you say you followed? Don't you know what the most important lesson is? That pleasure ends in murder and death? There is nothing greater than killing for pleasure. When it comes down to it, do you want to reach a solution or don't you?

BARON: I've already told you I'm not a proper libertine. I fall in love easily.

VOICE: The person who kills during an orgy, kills for pleasure. And of all the people there, you were the one who most desired the young creature. Weren't you?

BARON: I've already told you I'm innocent! I don't remember anything.

VOICE: You're just made for the prosecutor. If they'd called me as a witness for the prosecution, they wouldn't have needed to waste time. Your head would be marked for the chop.

BARON: I swear I'm innocent.

VOICE: That's not much. At the start, you seemed more intelligent to me. Your word's not enough. You spent the night in the arms of Morpheus and now you want everyone to believe in your reason?

You want them to be convinced you didn't kill anyone? You'd better change your argument, pal. You yourself told me at the beginning you needed to know who had died to discover the murderer.

BARON: And now I know. They killed Martine. She's the victim.

VOICE: If she's the victim, you're the main suspect. In an orgy, anyone who kills kills for pleasure.

BARON: It wasn't me!

VOICE: You don't know. You can't know. You were unconscious. As well as being a murderer, you've missed the opportunity of enjoying the crime while you were in control of your faculties.

BARON: I'm innocent!

VOICE: Let's try another route. What motive could the count and the baroness have had to kill the maid?

BARON: And how should I know? You yourself say they're mad. Jealousy, I don't know. The count might have got jealous. He fancied the maid. Who can swear that he hadn't already had her? She was the only maid he had in the house.

VOICE: Wasn't it you yourself who asked to be judged without the truth of feelings being taken

into account? And what could the baroness have to
do with any possible jealousy of the count because
of the maid?

BARON: She was used by the count. A plaything
in his hands. He might have told her that I would
be capable of killing her to get the maid, that
Martine had that power over men. He didn't want
me to free Martine from his yoke and convinced the
baroness to appear at the château that night.

VOICE: Wanting to take part in the orgy?

BARON: He used her. He always had a lot of influence over her. Even more after the Terror. She owed
him her life. As I did. She said he'd saved her from
the list of suspects when she came back from exile
or wherever it was she'd been, to marry me. She
couldn't refuse him a favour. It might all have been
a show. That's why the pastilles knocked me out.
He had to make me unconscious to kill the maid
and put the blame on me. He asked for the baroness's
help. Can't you see that's the most plausible account
of what happened?

VOICE: Then why didn't they disappear, leaving
you alone with the body?

BARON: Because, if they'd fled, they'd have aroused suspicion.

VOICE: But, since they stayed, why didn't they serve as prosecution witnesses? All they needed to say was that they'd seen you killing the maid for your head to be marked for the chop.

BARON: They couldn't, because they'd be accomplices. If they were there, why didn't they stop me? It was two against one, they could have stopped me. They used the same pretext: they said they were unconscious because of the pastilles, and hadn't seen anything.

VOICE: The same pretext? Is that the way you want to escape from the court's examination? The same pretext as yours? You mean to say that the sleep brought on by the aniseed pastilles was a pretext?

BARON: It was a manner of speaking. I put it badly.

VOICE: Very badly. We'll not get anywhere that way. When it comes down to it, do you want to know the truth or not? Sometimes, it seems to me that it would be better to leave things as they are, in ignorance.

BARON: I'm saying it wasn't me!

VOICE: I think you must have understood by now that that phrase means absolutely nothing. You can't speak for yourself. There's nothing more fragile than words spoken in a waking state, all the more when people act when they're asleep.

BARON: Fine. Then what's to be done?

VOICE: You must doubt all certainties. Even the most basic ones. You have to hand yourself over to me, dear sir. Answer my questions, take me as a guide, and don't resist. I'll tell you all I heard in the refectory. Together we'll try to reach a conclusion. But you'll have to listen to me first. You'll have to submit to me.

BARON: Sorry, but I think I'm seeing things again. It's horrible! I've the impression I glimpsed you in the shadows. And again, in my vision you . . . are black as pitch, as well as . . .

VOICE: I've already said it's impossible to see anything here! At the beginning, you seemed an intelligent man to me. This isn't the moment to despair, but to focus your mind on what's most important. You spoke to me of the revenge in the eyes of the maid when you met her, when you invited her to visit you in the château. Revenge for what?

BARON: For her status, of course. Probably on the count.

VOICE: Well, the count must have had some reason to kill her, according to your hypothesis, and jealousy, what you suggested, doesn't seem enough. You said you need the opinion of someone who doesn't believe in feelings. Everything is a convention. Only pleasure and the instincts are real. The count didn't kill the maid out of jealousy. In the refectory, while the baroness was saying over and over: 'What a nightmare! What a nightmare!', if that woman with the fiery hair is really the baroness, he, the count, was trying to convince her that they had no choice. 'She did it on purpose. You saw the countess's clothes. She had one of the countess's dresses on!' And, at that moment, the baroness stopped repeating her mantra to ask him, in an irritated voice, to shut his mouth. She said, sharply: 'You'd better think twice before you make your comments, if you still think you can escape the guillotine with your contacts.' Probably you're right when you say they must have used the pretext that they were unconscious, under the effect of the pastilles. Only you can't repeat that to the court, because your own alibi would be useless. They know that the best thing for them is not to have seen anything. It wouldn't shock me if they'd also said to the court, like you, that they didn't know who the victim was, and that's why they too were committed. We have to know what motive they had to kill her.

BARON: Martine! I can hear her voice telling me: 'I want to be with you. I want to prove that God doesn't exist' in the carriage on the way to what was left of the château. The same thing as the baroness. The same thing all the men and all the women in the world say. Even if it's only once in their lives. When they are more alive than ever. She couldn't know that the count was expecting her. And I had no way of warning her. But I wasn't to blame. I can hear her voice saying 'I want to submit myself to your pleasures', as she watched me leave the count's lands. She was for me. The worst thing is her having died without experiencing pleasure.

VOICE: Who said that's so?

BARON: I didn't have time to deflower her.

VOICE: Who can swear to that? You don't remember anything. And who can swear the count didn't rape her before he killed her?

BARON: No! Martine! I hear her voice saying 'I'm on my way. I want to give myself', in the carriage, with the countess's dress, without knowing that the count was waiting there to punish her. It's as if I'd set a trap for her! As if I'd betrayed her!

VOICE: Doesn't it seem strange to you that the count and the baroness have taken all the trouble to come all the way from wherever it was . . .

BARON: From Bordeaux.

VOICE: . . . from Bordeaux to punish a maid?

BARON: You can see how strong her desire for vengeance for her condition was. For them, it was unthinkable that a maid . . .

VOICE: A maid . . .

BARON: That she should give herself to me, and dressed as the countess to boot. You should have seen when she came into what was left of the salons in the château, after the count, and with her head lowered. She was even more beautiful when she was punished. The count robbed me of that pleasure, and that's unpardonable too.

VOICE: It seems you're getting closer to the truth. They came all the way from Bordeaux not to participate in one of your orgies, but because they were determined not to let you punish the maid. They sent you to sleep so you couldn't deflower her. Are you following me, baron? They came all the way from Bordeaux because they were worried about her. By that logic, they had no reason to kill her. That would be a contradiction. So, you're the guilty one. You killed her!

BARON: No! How could I have killed her if I was asleep?

VOICE: And who said you were?

BARON: I'm telling you!

VOICE: That's not enough.

BARON: They're lying! They didn't come all the way from Bordeaux to the château to save her from me. They couldn't have cared less. Aristocrats, even when they're reformed, don't care about maids!

VOICE: Ah, now you've got where I wanted.

BARON: What are you talking about?

VOICE: Aristocrats don't care about maids.

BARON: But I swear to you I was in love. With me, she would discover pleasure.

VOICE: Aristocrats don't care about maids. They've got other things to do.

BARON: What are you suggesting? I've told you I loved her.

VOICE: I can say the same about the count and the baroness.

BARON: What do you mean?

VOICE: Why couldn't they love the maid too?

BARON: Come on, where are you trying to take me with your syllogisms? You know very well they couldn't love her as I did.

VOICE. Why not?

BARON: You want to tell me . . . You're insinuating that the two of them, my cousin and my own chaste wife . . . that the two of them subjected the maid to bacchanalian orgies?

The Voice lets out an immense guffaw. The baron, embarrassed, puts on an unconvincing laugh, trying to go along with him.

BARON: Sorry, master, but I've had that vision again . . .

VOICE: How can you have visions if you can't see beyond your nose? How many times am I going to have to repeat your own phrase, that nobles don't concern themselves with maids, to make you understand at last? Nobles only concern themselves with other nobles. How many times must I repeat that to make you understand?

BARON: Understand what? The count was always on my side. It was he who introduced the baroness to me. They were friends. What are you hinting at now? Are you trying to say that the count and the baroness . . . ? Is that it?

VOICE: By the looks of things, you're halfway there. I'm sorry to have to confirm that, from what I could see in the refectory, they really are together, the count and the baroness, together as man and wife, and probably they always have been. Why did the count introduce you to the baroness? Because it suited him. And her too.

BARON: What are you trying to say?

VOICE: Why did she disappear for seven months

straight after she knew you, if she was in love as you say?

BARON: It was a way of seducing me!

VOICE: A way of seducing me! A way of seducing me!

BARON: She knew of my libertine past. She knew she had no chance with me unless she had a strategy. I wasn't going to get married just like that, after so many years refusing marriage. It was an excuse she invented to convince me.

VOICE: Exactly. An excuse. Try to think of anything a woman might hide for seven months.

BARON: What are you trying to tell me now?

VOICE: The obvious. The thing only you don't want to see.

BARON: But that's not possible!

VOICE: Do the sums yourself.

BARON: It's not possible!

VOICE: Fifteen years.

BARON: My God! Fifteen years!

VOICE: That's what always happens. When things get tight, they appeal to God.

BARON: A child!

VOICE: Seven months and then fifteen years.

BARON: How didn't I see it?

VOICE: Everyone sees what he wants.

BARON: How is it I never saw the same features, the same little breasts pressed into the silver corset?

VOICE: Not only the little breasts, but the two-months-gone stomach pressed in by the baroness's silver corset. It was no accident the count presented you to her. She was already two months pregnant. You were useful to both of them. You were the alibi they needed to stay together after the child was born. They could get rid of the child of their adultery, they could give her to a convent, but they needed to prevent suspicion with a marriage.

BARON: I've played the role of a clown! I didn't see a thing when I met her.

VOICE: You still don't. You're a slave to your feelings. You were their last chance. From then on it would be more difficult to trick even a blind man. She wasn't just getting too old. She had to get married for other reasons. Like most people, she needed a façade to hide what her instincts had forced her to do.

BARON: I can't see anything anywhere.

VOICE: Of course you can't, in this darkness. And perhaps it's better that way.

BARON: You're saying that to console me.

VOICE: To spare you. Sometimes, sight is a terrible thing. If you could see me, you probably wouldn't be able to bear my presence. Some even go mad.

BARON: How could I have been so blind? Seven months were enough. She never emigrated, minx! She'd have gone to the guillotine if she'd returned. She never left France. She hid her pregnancy in some convent or other, just as she did the child, who ended up escaping before the mother superior could use her. And if it hadn't been for that sudden refusal of sex after the marriage, I'd have found out.

VOICE: They hid the girl for fifteen years.

BARON: The same little breasts pressed together by the silver corset.

VOICE: You weren't that blind, in the end.

BARON: What a nightmare!

VOICE: That's the same thing I heard the mother say in the refectory.

BARON: The minx!

VOICE: You also saw the revenge in the girl's eyes.

BARON: No wonder!

VOICE: That's right. Fifteen years.

BARON: Why didn't I see it before?

VOICE: It was better that way. There were other things too you didn't understand.

BARON: I've understood everything. I've been used by the count. He saved me from the Revolution because he needed me. Now I know why they appeared at the château.

VOICE: Do you understand?

BARON: But of course. They couldn't let the revenge be carried out. When she submitted to me, Martine would avenge us both at the same time. How is it I didn't understand at the time that she's decided to give herself up as a sacrifice for such a valiant cause? What pleasure it would have been to deflower her for a cause like that! She wanted to avenge herself for the humiliation that they'd imposed on the two of us for the fifteen years when they kept her hidden with the nuns and then as a maid, and kept me as a blind clown. And all because of a rotten morality. Everything's beginning to make sense.

VOICE: Everything?

BARON: Everything the count did for me. All the advice he gave me. Why he was never with the countess and why the baroness was never with me in those fifteen years. Why I never knew of Martine's existence until that day. Why she accepted my proposal so promptly. Why she wanted to come to the château. To avenge herself. And why they appeared so soon after. Why the baroness wanted to take part in one of my orgies for the first time. Why she wouldn't allow any prostitute to take part. Why the count persuaded me to obey the baroness's sudden whims. Why they brought what they called an aphrodisiac!

VOICE: Why?

BARON: They wanted to get rid of the two of us at the same time, accusing me of the murder. That's what they call the love of a father and mother? They're monsters! They've killed their own daughter! My God!

VOICE: How many times must I repeat that the name of God only serves lazy people who end up getting lost on that shortcut to unreason?

BARON: And aren't they monstrous assassins?

VOICE: Certainly.

BARON: Their own daughter!

VOICE: In the refectory, I heard the count say to the baroness that now the girl was a long way away, there was no way back. It'd be better to forget!

BARON: She's in heaven! She's an angel!

VOICE: Everyone sees what they want to.

BARON: What are you hinting at this time? Let's have a minimum of respect for the dead! She was a virgin. And then there's the scandal of her revenge. If I'd deflowered her, she'd have given me the chance to revenge myself for everything they've done to me. How they've used me. (*horrified*) Master!

VOICE: I've already asked you not to call me that. Now what is it?

BARON: The vision, again.

VOICE: And what do you want me to tell you?

BARON: That it's not true.

VOICE: What?

BARON: What I thought I saw.

VOICE: Everyone sees what they want to.

BARON: I must be hallucinating. It must be normal.

After all, they killed their own daughter just to incriminate me. And how can anyone fail to react to that? They're capable of anything. They couldn't allow her to take her revenge on them, the more so in the way she'd thought up, using me as an accomplice. Their pride is greater than their love. They had no pity. How horrible!

VOICE: They had no pity. That's the least you can say.

BARON: And she had to pay for what they'd done, for the responsibility they'd never admitted to!

VOICE: She must be feeling very lonely.

BARON: What do you mean?

VOICE: Wasn't it you who said just now that she's in heaven? And that she was an angel? An angel among so many sinners?

BARON: This is no time for irony.

VOICE: It seems you still haven't realised that you don't set the time here.

BARON: How could I be so stupid? Why did I accept the pastilles? I could have saved the girl. How did I fall into such a simple trap? I should have suspected as soon as they appeared at the château. They wouldn't have come all the way from Bordeaux for nothing.

VOICE: Everyone sees what they want to.

BARON: (*yelling*) But I can't see anything here! I want to get out of here at once! Where are they? They'll pay for what they've done! For the first time in their lives, they'll pay! Get me out of here at once! Get me out of here!

VOICE: Don't be silly. There's no point in shouting. I'm here at your side; I can hear you.

BARON: But someone needs to do something! I need to tell the court what happened.

VOICE: They already know.

BARON: And why? Why don't they let me out of here?

VOICE: Because they can't.

BARON: But I'm innocent!

VOICE: That's what they all say.

BARON: I want to see them!

VOICE: You can't, I've already said.

BARON: I know, I know! They're under observation. Waiting for what?

VOICE: What everyone's waiting for.

BARON: Will they be executed, then?

VOICE: I wouldn't go that far.

BARON: But that's what they deserve for killing their own daughter. And if the baroness says it's a nightmare, it's maybe because she's repentant. Perhaps she'll confess the crime. And then they'll have to free me.

VOICE: I doubt it.

BARON: And they're going to leave me here for the rest of my life?

VOICE: I wouldn't necessarily put it that way.

BARON: And how would you put it if you were in my place? Come on! How?

VOICE: There are things you still haven't understood.

BARON: Don't be condescending. I might have been stupid and blind once, but now everything's quite clear.

VOICE: Really?

BARON: And anyway, what does it matter, now that she's dead?

VOICE: Dead?

BARON: I could have saved Martine.

VOICE: Now, she's far away. It's irreversible.

BARON: Like the angels in heaven.

VOICE: I'm trying to be patient, but your blindness is irritating.

BARON: If at least there was a little light in here. I'm tired.

VOICE: Tired? But it's only the beginning.

BARON: Nothing makes any sense now that she's dead. Perhaps if I went the same way she has. And left behind the unjust, petty world of men. You might be able to help me. All I need is a rope. Could you get hold of a rope for me, since you have access to every wing of the asylum?

VOICE: It's no use. There's no escape from here.

BARON: You haven't understood. I'm ready to end my life.

The Voice lets out a guffaw.

VOICE: I've understood perfectly. I think you're the one who hasn't understood.

BARON: I want to be with Martine.

VOICE: It's incredible how, when things get tight,

all of you, even the proudest of libertines, begin to believe in the angels of heaven.

BARON: It's better than staying in this quagmire.

VOICE: Voilà! The same thing the count said to the baroness about the maid.

BARON: Martine. She's their daughter.

VOICE: Martine, then! It's all the same. It's better to send her away from this quagmire, so she'll not be defiled by this filth.

BARON: This is all getting ridiculous. I asked you to help me. You're no longer being logical, master. All this is absurd. You want to convince me with a tawdry argument that the two of them killed their daughter to save her? How can you believe that? And that they got rid of the body to save her reputation, so that her honour would not be besmirched? Only so that the news that she had been killed during an orgy at château Lagrange shouldn't get about?! Is that it?

VOICE: That's not what I said. You're interpreting. Whenever they interpret, people lose themselves down these shortcuts. Nobody ever said she'd been murdered.

BARON: What are you saying?! Then Martine's alive?!

VOICE: That's the way it looks.

BARON: God be praised!

VOICE: You disappoint me.

BARON: But didn't they say, in the refectory? . . .

VOICE: That now she was a long way off.

BARON: Ah! . . .

VOICE: On the same night, after you'd swallowed the pastilles, they put her on board a ship going where no one would have any more news of her.

BARON: But of course! They made her disappear to incriminate me, and as the body hasn't yet been found, there are no proofs, and the court decided to keep them in the asylum. We're all saved!

VOICE: You're an optimist, baron.

BARON: What you've just said is reason for a celebration.

VOICE: Is it?

BARON: Martine is alive and all we have to do is prove it for them to free me and get on a ship too and find her, wherever she is.

VOICE: No one gets out of here.

BARON: But there's been no crime! There's been no murder!

VOICE: No one's said there hasn't been.

BARON: It's because they don't know she's alive. Because the count and the baroness did everything on purpose to incriminate me. They set up the whole imposture. They left me unconscious in the château and accused me, all the more with the count's contacts and so many people wanting to get their revenge on a provincial nobleman like me. What they didn't think was they'd be taken as suspects as well. And now they're down a cul-de-sac. To save their own skin, they'll have to confess they've hidden their daughter. And that way, without wanting to, they'll free me too. It's all a matter of time, the time they'll manage to put up with being imprisoned here without saying anything. That's it! That's it! Just the time they manage to put up with it without saying anything.

VOICE: It's incredible how you still refuse to see. The only problem, my dear man, is that there has in fact been a murder.

BARON: (*silence*) Master? . . . I must be going mad.

Help me. I'm certain I've seen you, but I don't want to believe.

VOICE: What in?

BARON: No. It must be a hallucination. It can only be a hallucination.

VOICE: Everyone sees what they want to – or what they can.

BARON: Why isn't there even a chink of light anywhere?

VOICE: It's better for you.

BARON: (*shrinking back*) When all's said and done, who are you? Who's there?! (*silence*) If it's not the Marquis de Sade, then who is it? What do you want of me? (*silence*) Why since they arrested me have they been talking a language I don't understand? Why are they calling me by another name? Why do I only understand what you say? What do you mean when you say there was a murder? Why can't I get out if I didn't kill anyone? (*silence*) I'm pouring with sweat. Look! My shirt's soaking. Why is it so hot? And even so, I'm still shaking. Why am I having these hallucinations? I'm afraid. Why don't you tell me who you are? What do you want to spare me

from? (*silence*) If Martine wasn't murdered, then . . .
who was? (*silence*) Why don't you answer? (*silence*)
Master? Who died? Who's the dead one? What is this
place? Why isn't there a chink of light anywhere?

ACT TWO

A blinding white light. Two men dressed in white, a black man and a white man, are walking along a white-tiled corridor. They hear shouts at the far end, in another language. Someone, it seems, desperately wants to get out of there.

THE BLACK MAN IN WHITE TO THE WHITE MAN IN WHITE: Where are we? You can't take anything with you from this world, so make the most of it. That's what he keeps on saying. You remember the crime. Everyone does. It was some time ago. It was in all the papers. From the beginning, everyone knew who the murderer was. There wasn't the least doubt. Even if it was never proved. You didn't have to be very bright. But the world wants proof. He ended up confessing – within his own reasoning, of course, which they didn't think at all reasonable. Because they didn't manage to find the killers. There were no proofs. It was only the police who didn't suspect the obvious right from the beginning; they nearly let him escape. If it hadn't been for the newspaper article, at the airport. They had to give free rein to the investigation, to get where everyone had suspected anyhow, before they could make a decision. Fools. Their luck, or rather his downfall, was his going into that newspaper stall. He was already on his way back, in the airport, when he saw the news and lost his head. He told the whole story. They couldn't let him go after the confession, even if he'd been taken for a madman. While they had no proof. And while they waited for it, he ended up being forgotten here. The important thing isn't who was the murderer, but the paradox of the murder itself. He had his own wife killed so he could commit another crime that never was or will be committed. Because, with his wife's death, and even before that, with the very thought of killing his wife, though he didn't know or even suspect it, thinking that that way he made his plan possible, he was already committing suicide. They were a curious

couple. Not that she was any better than him. They
deserved each other. Neither of them was any good.
But there was one extraordinary thing about that
marriage. They married in a chapel on top of a hill,
as simple as simple can be, in the south of France,
in the town where he'd been born and where at the
beginning of the nineteenth century, so it seems, a
baron laid on orgies inspired by the Marquis de
Sade. A libertine writer whose central philosophy
was treachery. Six months after they were married,
they found out she couldn't have children. They
realised that love doesn't outlast time, love ends,
and they made an explicit pact which, usually, in
the general run of marriages, destroys them by
remaining unsaid. They decided the best thing was
to establish a relationship based on treachery and
horror. Horror instead of love. A marriage based on
a game of horrors, because, as he keeps saying during
his attacks, horror doesn't die, unlike love. Only
horror can keep a marriage alive, on the principle
of treachery, according to the philosophy of this
libertine baron. Each of the spouses plays a joke on
the other, successively and in turn. It's what they

learned to call, in a game restricted to the two of them, the 'fear of Sade'. A reference to the famous marquis, of course; it seems plain that it was under Sade's influence that the baron created his own peculiar philosophy. You know. The one who's more afraid loses. That was the game. Whoever got afraid, lost. 'Fear of Sade'. And when he ordered his wife to be killed, paradoxically, he lost. They went on playing tricks on one another, each one more horrible than the last, and that way they intended to stay together until death, as they'd promised in the eyes of the Church. They went on playing tricks on each other to keep, as far as possible, the oath they'd taken in the little chapel on the top of the hill, in the south of France, as simple as simple can be. Only the business didn't last long. Even treachery has its rules, and he cheated. He wanted to put the cart before the horse. He tried to bring death forward, to kill his wife before she killed him. He got scared. And in this game whoever gets scared, loses. It might seem paradoxical to you, and to me too, but when she died, she won. When she died, she terrified him. You can get an idea from his screams. Between one joke and another, she ended up saying something she shouldn't have. She didn't exactly say that she'd found out the crime he was planning. It was he who interpreted her that way. She was more ambiguous and enigmatic. It's most likely she only wanted to provoke him, to exacerbate what she thought was an attack of jealousy. Maybe she was just trying him on. She only put into words what was already in his head. Or perhaps not even that. Maybe she didn't know anything. But that was the way he understood it. He thought she'd discovered the crime he was planning. Not the crime against herself, of course – that came later, and because of what she said – but against the client. After those words, it was his turn to play a trick on her. And she knew she couldn't escape when she agreed to the journey he proposed to her, just like that, with the lame excuse that they needed some peace, some holiday, just the two of them. She might not have known, but at least she suspected, if it was only because of his behaviour. That's why she planned everything before she died. She planned to play a trick on her husband with her own death, since it was inevitable, a trick even more

horrible than death itself. She would leave as her
inheritance another motive for horror, and this time
he would be inconsolable. She didn't want to die
without getting her own back. She didn't want to
take the 'fear of Sade' to the grave with her. She left
her vengeance ready. And there's no way of knowing at what point she realised and took the decision,
to what degree she'd got everything set from the
day she said those words to him, when he thought
she'd found out what he was planning, and preferred
to have her killed to having to live with the suspicion, however remote the chances of her really having
found anything out. They deserved one another. It's
no accident they were married. They met in a firm
in the north of France. She worked as an account-
ant and he was a legal consultant. They were a perfect
pair. She was a wizard at numbers, which was just
what he was no good at; he studied law because he
couldn't do anything else. She'd always done sums
since she was little. And it would be a euphemism
to say he'd never been any good at maths. He just
hadn't the gift for it. It's not that he was stupid, but
since childhood his capacity for abstraction had never

been anything to write home about. He only understood the four basic algebraic operations on the day he translated them into everyday language and realised that multiplying two by two, for instance, simply meant twice two, a duplication of two. He understood algebra through semantics, which in its turn was not the woman's strong point, so much so that she signed her own death warrant when she said those words without measuring the consequences. As long as it lasted, they were complementary. Numbers and meaning. They pulled off a hoax on the firm, a first-class swindle, a hoax based on confidence so they couldn't be caught, and went to live in the south of France, where he'd been born. They were married right there, in a little country chapel, with the ruins of the libertine baron's château in the background. A discreet ceremony, only for those closest to them, hardly anyone, and his family. She preferred not to invite her own family. Only her sister. She hadn't been speaking to her parents for years. The idea of substituting horror for love wasn't alien to her. She might well have been inspired by her own childhood, and her own family. It was putting hunger and the urge to eat together when he introduced her to the collected works of the baron. Because he was a fan of the libertine literature of the end of the eighteenth century. It was through him she discovered the baron and his philosophy of treachery. In one of his books, a moralising novel in dialogue form, the baron recounted how he had avenged himself on the wife who was betraying him: he deflowered the illegitimate daughter she'd had by his cousin. Because, according to the baron's philosophy, only treachery liberates. Treachery is repaid with treachery. Nothing could be more appropriate, then, than betraying the conventions of a morality which attempts in its turn to be false to nature. And the baron could think of nothing more treacherous than depraving the illegitimate daughter of his own adulterous wife to avenge himself on her and her demure maternal hypocrisy. He's a writer who proposes a world in which virtues and values are turned upside down, inside out, where evil is good, and treachery is honour. A world of anti-virtues, as the only way of escaping from the hypocrisy of religion and the limitations of human conventions in the name of the truth of the instincts. A world of anti-virtues for a philosophy. An anti-humanism at the beginning of the nineteenth century. And it's no accident that she was delighted when her husband showed her the collected works of the baron and said to her: 'We are here to prove God doesn't exist. No effort should be spared, no means excluded in this undertaking. Our lives will prove God doesn't exist, or we wouldn't be what we are.' They also came across a world of anti-virtues after they went up the hill on foot to the little chapel. The simplest thing in the world. The marriage was a way of sealing the alliance they made when they pulled off the first hoax, which left the boss with his hands tied when he wanted to give the police their names, since they were only able to act thanks to his complete confidence in them. They came out clean and with money in their pockets. The boss was completely to blame, for he had delegated all power to them, and any naming of them, as well as being useless from the criminal point of view – for there was no way of pinning the blame on them – would only be a complete, shameful revelation of

the fraud and of his own naiveté. They were careful with the money from the hoax. They didn't want
to attract attention. They intended to pull off
others, if only to prove God doesn't exist. The world
needs proof. They were a perfect pair of swindlers.
They had their lives in front of them. She was a
wizard with numbers. Straight after they were
married, he opened an office in the small town. Six
months before discovering she couldn't have children, which was the sign, and also the beginning of
the game and their downfall. They realised straight
away only horror could keep them together. They
realised they would only have a chance by indulging
in horror. They ended up linking this horror to the
libertine baron's philosophy of treachery. Before
horror and treachery could become established and
control the relationship in spite of them — as happens
in the general run of marriages, according to the
baron — she proposed the game to him, inspired by
the baron's philosophy and by her own childhood.
At the start it was fun. He let her go out in the car
in the early morning after he'd emptied the brake
fluid in the middle of the night, which she only

noticed when she put her foot down on the pedal, and, avoiding a cart, lost control on a twisty but fortunately flat and near-empty road which went through a maize field, where she ended up in total chaos, though without any serious injury. She crashed against a tree and when they came to her assistance they found her laughing out loud to herself when she realised what had happened. She, in her turn, hired two lads, members of the party of the extreme right whose meeting the couple used to attend, to mug him when he came home alone one stifling night, after work, while she was in the supermarket. Two months later, he abandoned her in a small yacht they'd rented, out at sea, pretending he'd been drowned, while she, who could hardly swim or sail, adrift in the boat, was desperately trying to get help on a radio which had been purposely broken. Until another boat came to save her. She forged a summons from the Ministry of Finance, which he got in the mail, accusing him of tax evasion. And he went as far as to appear at the appointed day and time, terrified, after a good deal of hesitation, for fear that if they'd discovered the tip of the iceberg, they might find the submerged part; he only realised he'd been tricked when the receptionist told him she didn't know of any employee with the name of the person who had signed the summons. And there, on the spot, in front of the Ministry of Finance receptionist, he laughed out loud as she had done after the accident in the middle of the maize field. They knew how to enjoy themselves. The game was a school of fear. A never-ending test. And, in their own way, you could even say they were happy. Until she said those words and he broke the rules and brought her death forward. Not that they might not die, as a result of a trick with a greater risk of violence, for example, or by some mistake in the plans, that was part of it, but chance had always been a fundamental element. It wouldn't have been right to get rid of chance. He had planned every detail of her death, so she couldn't escape. It was the only way of being able to carry out the rest of his plan, so he thought, still completely unconsciously, without realising that all he had to do was eliminate her to ruin every-thing. In this game between them, she might create problems at any moment, and he didn't want to risk anything, at least not this time. He couldn't. He wanted to kill a client and didn't need accomplices. He didn't want to leave witnesses. The only thing he didn't know was how she'd found out. If she really had found out, as those words made him think she had. Also, he couldn't imagine what she might leave to be said only at the moment of death; she might avenge herself when she was murdered, and he'd be caught completely unprepared. One night, when he returned home after an untimely, unexplained crisis which to those who didn't know them might even look like jealousy and maybe the wife had interpreted that way, she was waiting for him in the living-room, as usual. It was a stone house on top of a hill, like the little chapel, with a view over the valley and the ruins of the baron's castle, a house they'd bought with the money from the first swindle, when they realised they were made for one another. A house she decorated 'in the American style', as she liked to say to please her husband, whose dream was to move one day to Chicago, the land of gangsters and limitless opportunity, at least

that was what he proclaimed in the first months of
the marriage; he was always consorting with the
worst people in the town, before they discovered
she couldn't have children. It was when he realised
that he'd stopped finding it funny, and it wasn't just
from what she said. He even slapped her in the house
at the mere mention of the phrase 'in the American
style' about the decoration, in the presence of a
couple of guests they'd recently got to know at the
meetings of the party of the extreme right, who left
in a hurry, out of sheer embarrassment. And before
the horror took over, she decided to take the initiative and propose to her husband this game, which
to you and me might seem insane, inspired by what
she had gone through in childhood, but also under
the influence of the libertine baron, at first sight
with the single aim of saving their marriage. If she
was going to be hit, then it might as well be with
her own consent, in a game. That way they would
take turns in the roles of victim and torturer. If it
would save the marriage. They even laughed at the
pretext. But not for long. Only till the night when
she was waiting for him in the living-room, after

he'd had a crazy attack of jealousy, which made no
sense at all at that stage of the proceedings, when
he came home without saying a word. She said she
had something to say to him. And she spoke in the
same way she referred to the décor of the house in
front of the guests: 'in the American style'. She said
just what he didn't want to hear at that moment.
Her eyes shining, and with a glass of whisky in her
hand, she said: 'For you, the best thing would be if
he didn't exist, he's your weak point'. She didn't say
anyone's name, as if she read her husband's thoughts,
and at that moment he could only imagine she'd
found out. Though he couldn't understand how. His
whole brain was taken up with the plan to get rid
of the client. He knew she might just be trying it
on, to put him to the test and terrify him. She might
be talking about something else. But he couldn't live
with the suspicion, now that everything was real.
He couldn't let her find out and get in the way of
his plans. He couldn't allow himself to get into her
power, to be threatened by her. And what if, in any
future reversal of the game, she decided to inform
on him to the police to terrify him even more? That

was the only thing the wife said, her eyes shining, and with a glass of whisky in her hand: 'For you, the best thing would be if he didn't exist, he's your weak point'. And it was enough. It was only of secondary importance, whether she knew or not. It hardly mattered whether she knew about her husband's plans to kill his client or not. He couldn't go ahead, with that on his mind. With a single sentence, she'd brought about her own death. What he couldn't suspect was that, in a certain sense, this was a form of suicide. He couldn't know that perhaps there was nothing involuntary or unconscious about what his wife did. It's possible she was tired, or that she had to put him in check, and check-mate him only with her own death. Perhaps she had no strength or imagination left in her. Because it was a game of the imagination. Perhaps she'd simply felt the moment of the final trick arrive; what's certain is that she played like an actress in a gangster movie she saw on television while she was doing accounts, always doing accounts, 'in the American style': sitting on the living-room sofa with her eyes shining and a glass of whisky in her hand. He pretended he hadn't heard and changed the subject. He didn't ask 'who d'you mean, he?' He didn't change expression. He changed the subject. He was imperturbable. She pretended to think he hadn't heard, and replied to what he asked her now about something else nothing to do with what she'd said. He knew as well as she did that the next step would be his, it was his turn, the next trick was his. She knew he had heard the sentence and taken it in. He knew that she knew he had heard the sentence and taken it in. And that she was waiting for his reaction, for him to get even. But they acted as if they didn't know, so that the game could go on. The next month, he came home with two air tickets, even though he had a fear of flying, and said the two of them were in need of a holiday. 'But isn't it a dangerous place?', the wife asked, 'in the American style', sitting on the living-room sofa with her eyes shining and a glass of whisky in her hand, referring to the destination he'd deliberately chosen. 'Isn't it a city with a high crime index? Are you sure it isn't risky?' And he swore they would have a wonderful week, that, after a lot of thought, he'd chosen it among all the cities in the world. It seemed to him the most suitable. And she smiled, sitting on the sofa with her eyes shining and a glass of whisky in her hand. That was the way they played it. The best victim is the one who pleases the torturer, who enjoys the role of victim. And she deluded him so well. At no moment did she let him see that he would be the greatest victim of her death. Not for a moment. Only when it was already irreversible, when she was already dying and he couldn't do anything else to save himself from the 'fear of Sade' she was leaving him with. She was going to die 'in the American style', with a glint in her eyes and a smile on her lips. She looked at the tickets and asked him what they were going to do there. She'd heard that the city was hell on earth, and terribly hot. And he, pretending he believed in her objections, played his role too and tried to convince her, affectionately, that they needed a week's holiday, it was some time since they'd been together, just the two of them. And she pretended to give in. She'd already been persuaded a long time before he'd brought her the tickets. She already knew that if it wasn't here, it would be in Bangkok, in

Yemen or Istanbul, in some place or other she would have to disappear. She had to disappear ever since she said those words: 'For you, the best thing would be if he didn't exist, he's your weak point'. He pretended not to hear it, because he didn't even bother to ask 'Who d'you mean, he?' He knew that she might be trying it on or making a mistake, provoking him in connection with the apparent, unexpected attack of jealousy in the afternoon. He knew she might be talking about something else, or even someone else, and not the client. He knew she might not know anything about it. But he couldn't expose his flank. He couldn't even risk bothering to ask 'Who d'you mean, he?' She'd invited death with those words. The only thing he didn't know was that, through her death, he was the one that would die. They boarded the plane at night and got here in the morning. He was calm, or at least feigning calm, in spite of his fear of planes. He was very attentive to her the whole night through. And she was calling his bluff. Her life to prove God doesn't exist. It's very probable she was tired. Tired of thinking up new horror-games. She'd put all her cards on this last one. She knew it would be the last. He did too. Only that he thought the last throw of the dice would be his and not hers. That was why he was calm. They went through passport control, through customs, and when they got out with their luggage, a man speaking French and with a sheet of paper on which the couple's surname was printed was waiting for them in the airport arrivals area. 'See how easy it was? I've got everything organised. From now on, they look after everything,' said the husband to the wife in a fatherly tone, which she returned with her smile 'in the American style'. The man accompanied them to the car outside. She got in first, then her husband. The man who had met them and the driver looked after the cases. Then they too got into the car. The husband gave them the hotel address. But they went off in the opposite direction. She wasn't the first to notice. She was tired, and she'd handed herself over. She knew what her destiny was. Or suspected, at least. She'd won. It was up to him to give the sign. And that was what he did at a certain moment. He pretended to be suspicious and apprehensive. And it was only when she noticed his false nervousness that she emerged from her sleepiness and asked him what the matter was. It was at that moment, when the husband told her he thought they weren't going the right way, and while they were moving away from the centre of the city, going past shacks, filth and vacant lots, that she took on the role of victim and, getting suddenly nervous in her turn, asked the man who'd met them at the airport where they were going and got the fatal reply. He turned round and ordered the two of them to shut up, not 'in the American style', but in a sharp, brutal way which terrified her for the first time. That was the game, after all. This really was horror. However much everything was planned (as she had planned it, without her husband knowing, thinking he was in control of the situation), however much she might know where she was going, at bottom she never knew. There were always surprises, things that were unexpected. Like when the man who had met them at the airport raised his hand and clouted her in the face. And she, who had sat forward, on the edge of the seat to ask where they were going, flew back into the upholstery. The game was different here. She tried to open the door and fling herself out of the car. And then, when she saw she couldn't get out, she began to cry. She wept her heart out. She remembered her childhood, boarding school, her brothers in silence as they were beaten with a belt, the time she spent in her grandparents' house, her grandmother's death, her certainty that hell was right here, her first job and the operation she did with the first money she got, the first time she mutilated herself, the first of many. Without telling anyone, she persuaded a doctor to take her womb out, so that she would never have the chance of getting pregnant and putting a child into this hell, not even by some unhappy accident or if she weakened in her determination, for love or some other lie, not wanting to be at the mercy of chance, of love, or of the possibility of conflicting wishes, human beings are complex, human beings will invent anything to justify what can't be explained, they invent God and love, and with the first money she earned she put an end to the whole farce and the guilt of bringing someone else into the world to prove, like her, that God doesn't exist. She ended the whole lie, but without anyone finding out, so she wouldn't be called mad, so much so that she didn't even tell her husband, not even him, when they met at the firm and planned the embezzlement together, so they couldn't be caught, a plan based on the complete confidence of the boss, she doing the accounts and he the legal consultant, nor when they were partners in crime, nor when they were married in the chapel above the valley where he had been born, she didn't even tell him at the altar – she said the scar was from a Caesarean, spoke about a dead foetus – and it was only when he discovered the truth, and she saw that the horror could slip from her hands, that she decided to propose the game, since everything dies except horror. The foundation of the baron's philosophy. She wept for the marriage to which she'd decided only to invite her sister, the only one among the guests who understood what that marriage was, another act of self-mutilation, for life could only, *could only* be a series of self-mutilations to prove God doesn't exist, she wanted at least one of the guests to understand what was happening, and to be moved and feel pity for her. She wept for that last act of self-mutilation, in the car, at her husband's side, on the way to sacrifice and death. She wept for the expression on her sister's face in the church, she was the only member of her family she invited, lost, like her, among his relatives and the members of the party of the extreme right whose meetings they attended, the expression of someone who knows what everything means, another step in her self-mutilation. She wept when she realised the victory she'd won when she said those words to her husband : 'For you, the best thing would be if he didn't exist, he's your weak point', as if she were Lady Macbeth, 'in the American style', sitting on the sofa with her eyes shining and a glass of whisky in her hand, the victory of her death after a life of mutilations. She wept for fear as well, for the fear she would leave her husband as an inheritance when he finally understood what he'd done when he killed her, the fear that now was only hers and that in a few minutes' time, after she'd gone, would be his alone. The fear of everyone. The fear of those who are left. She wept bitterly over her thirty years and some. She wept for the look on

her husband's face when he discovered that she
hadn't had a womb since she was twenty. It was the
doctor in the small town who called him into his
surgery to tell him with embarrassment the reason
why his wife hadn't got pregnant after six months
of marriage. The husband, dumbfounded, asked the
doctor how that was possible, how it was she didn't
have a womb. And the doctor was forced to explain
to him. 'Is she mad, then?', was the only thing he
managed to ask the doctor, like a kind of answer.
'Is she mad, then?' before he went back home and
found her sitting on the sofa, with her eyes shining
and a glass of whisky in her hand. She wept for the
look on her husband's face when he got home with
the expression of someone who's just discovered the
trick that's been played on him. He might have got
excited over that mutilation with its philosophical
background, which fitted the baron's ideas so well.
He might have grasped everything from another point
of view. But he was horrified. She wept for the slap
she got, sitting on the sofa when she greeted him
that night, when she saw that they only had horror
left. She wept out of pity for him, that horrible man,

and her, that horrible woman. She wept bitterly for the two of them. Until the man on the front seat turned round again and gave her another good clout right on her cheek, shouting at her to stop crying or else. Now she was near death, she was desperate. The stage-set had gone. Security was gone. Pretence was gone. The certainty she would end up as the victor was gone. She began to scream, to struggle, and it was only when her husband gripped her that she came back to her senses, looking him in the eyes and seeing what he didn't see, that she was the winner – or could it be he was such a fool as to think she was going to accept everything he proposed to her without thinking of revenge? She saw all his self-satisfied lack of awareness in his eyes, but this didn't calm her down – rather she went into a catatonic state that at least anaesthetised her for the shock and prevented any reaction, even stopped her scream-ing. She was dumbstruck. That was what he thought later, with hindsight. Retrospectively, when he'd understood the trap he'd fallen into, the husband remembered seeing in her eyes, on the brink of death, what she had seen in his eyes, his unawareness, and that had made her go quiet. He'd set everything up, thinking she'd not see anything. He'd thought he could flout the rules of the game and bring her death forward without her seeing. He thought she'd go on playing as on other occasions, that she'd willingly submit, ignorant that this was the last time. He didn't see that, in a certain way, she'd programmed everything with those words: 'For you, the best thing would be if he didn't exist, he's your weak point'. What did she mean, he? But he didn't ask. He fell right into the trap. What did she mean, he? That was the question he should have asked. But he didn't. He deduced that she was talking about the client he was planning to rid himself of, as soon as he could, as soon as he had a chance. He thought she knew, that she'd read his thoughts. Because the only question hammering away in his head was how she'd found out. But it was the wrong question. What if she was talking about God? 'For you, the best thing would be if he didn't exist, he's your weak point'. Impertinence. Daring to cast doubt on the baron's philosophy. Or maybe she was talking about the baron himself. Do you understand? He understood with hindsight. He fell right into the trap of his mad wife's self-mutilations; she'd already married without a womb so as not to run the risk of putting a child into the world, another one to prove that God doesn't exist. That was the way the game had been going from the beginning, towards self-mutilation, how had he not seen that? He didn't see it while he held her down in the car and the man in the front seat turned round and slapped her again on the face with the full force of his hand. She looked at her husband, looked at the man in the front seat, at the driver, and now said nothing further. After everything she'd done against herself, she'd come to the end, and on top of that she was still taking with her the man who thought he was an executioner when he was nothing more than a victim. She'd come to the end, after all her self-mutilations, as the winner. She was going to die to destroy the life of the man who thought he could destroy hers. For the first time, with her own death, she could contemplate in someone else the destruction she'd kept for herself throughout her life, which was an advance, so he understood with hindsight, when he remembered his

wife looking silently out of the car window, after
she'd been slapped, while he held her down in the
car, as they went towards the place for the sacrifice
and the last scene of the game of horrors. Her eyes
were lost on the empty horizon, as if she were
resigned to her own fate, which she'd finally understood. The car veered onto an unmade road, and
after some ten minutes jolting through a more and
more desolate landscape, it stopped alongside thick
brushwood. The two in the front turned round and
looked at the husband. The husband looked at the
two in the front. He looked at his wife again. The
man that met them at the airport nodded his head
and the husband let go of his wife. The couple
looked at one another once more in a kind of good-
bye, before he told her to get out of the car and
run. 'Run!' he said. She opened the door but, before
she got out, with one foot already out of the car,
she turned to him and managed to say, 'in the
American style', which always rings false, as if she
was in a gangster movie and this was not her own
death, with her eyes shining and a smile on her lips:
'Checkmate!' He didn't understand straight away.

He thought she couldn't have been so naïve as to think she could still escape now. She began to run. The man who had met them at the airport opened the door, got out of the car, and with one foot out of the car, pointed the revolver at the woman's back, stumbling as she ran. The husband had lowered his head in the back seat. He didn't even bother to get out of the car and run too, even if only as a hammed-up attempt to pretend till the last moment that they were still in the same boat, he and his wife, after having made it quite clear they weren't, even if it was only so that she wouldn't carry the worst possible image of him with her in death. He lowered his head and shut his eyes at his wife's last word, which he couldn't get out of his head: checkmate, checkmate, checkmate, and suddenly he understood and shouted 'No!', with all his strength and at the same time as he heard the two sharp bangs and the noise of a body falling like an animal, flying, cutting through the undergrowth. 'No!' He got out of the car and fell on his knees, his mouth open and terror in his eyes. The man with the revolver turned the car round, came towards him and looked down at him. When the man lifted his face, he got a kick in the thigh and fell to one side, groaning. 'Chicken, huh?' asked the man with the revolver. 'At the last moment?' The Frenchman said nothing more. He didn't understand what the man was saying now, words in a strange language. He'd realised it was too late. He didn't yet know what was waiting for him, but he could imagine. He'd underestimated her. The man with the revolver gave him a push with the toe of his shoe and told him to get up, in French. 'Now it's your turn to run. Or are you sorry? Give me all your documents, credit cards, money'. The Frenchman took what he had out of his pockets and said the rest was in the case, pointing at the car. And the payment they'd agreed on, too. 'Get up!' shouted the man with the revolver and kicked him again, before he could react properly. 'So they won't suspect anything', said the man with the revolver, with a sarcastic smile. The Frenchman tried to get up, groaning. 'Get going!' ordered the man with the revolver, and he went, limping, in the opposite direction from his wife. Whatever happened, he didn't want to see her. He couldn't bear to see the body slumped on the ground. 'Not that way, idiot! The other side!', shouted the man, pointing the revolver in the direction where the woman had fallen. The Frenchman ran for some fifteen yards, groaning. Until he heard the shot and, at the same time, felt an awful pain in his leg, which made him fall to the ground, not very far from where his wife's body had flown, cutting through the bushes. Still on the ground, he heard the car rev up and disappear along the same unmade road.

He was one of the first clients he took on at his office. Seven months after he'd moved in. He was a computer technician who lived in an isolated farmhouse somewhere in the area. A strange character, who lived alone and came to him asking advice about a matter he said was extremely confidential, though he never revealed what it was. In the first two meetings, he asked several questions and then left, still without saying exactly why he wanted a lawyer. From the usual kind of questions, though a little enigmatic (for example: if he would undertake to follow the honour code to the letter in the defence of a client, whatever might happen), to other, less common ones (if he would take this case on even if he knew he would be pestered by the police and by the most contradictory desires). He was a very strange character, who irritated him and whom in other circumstances he'd have ignored, but not there, seven months after getting married and opening his office, and less than a year – still insufficient time for them to spend the money – after the swindle they carried out, he and his wife, on the firm where they'd met, the perfect swindle, based on confidence, so they couldn't be caught. This wasn't the moment to spoil everything. He'd acted carefully: he'd only bought the house from where he could see, far off, the ruins of the castle of the baron he venerated, and set up his office in a back street in the small town, a little room where the client appeared for the first time on a hot spring afternoon, in a hat, overcoat and dark glasses. With the exception of an old magistrate who kept on putting off his retirement, he had no competition in a thirty-mile radius. All the same, he still had no clients. And the computer technician, however strange it might seem, was one of the first to appear in seven months. He was a suspicious man. And quite right too, considering he was hiding a goldmine. Finally, at their third meeting, almost a month after the first, he told the lawyer he was employing him as intermediary in a transaction that would overturn the country's financial system. He was willing to pay a high price for his secret to be kept, for discretion. He wanted the lawyer to arrange a meeting with the board of the central bank, in Paris. For the first time, no longer able to control his irritation, he laughed at the client. 'Here's the number. Pick up the phone and ring. They're waiting', answered the computer technician, impassively. The lawyer stopped laughing and began looking at the client. He's the one who tells the story, when an attack comes on. It's always the same story: he took the number, lifted the phone off the hook and, when he was going to dial, he was interrupted once again by the client, who put his hand on the phone: 'First it's as well to know that from now on there's no way back. And that in a few hours this office may well be surrounded by the police. You must be made aware that you will be tempted by contradictory desires'. The lawyer had already gathered that it was a very risky case, though he didn't know its content. 'It's for your own good', the client had explained to him, justifying the fact that he couldn't reveal what it was about. Phone in hand, he dialled the number of the central bank in Paris, told the secretary who answered that he would like to have a meeting with the board of directors and was astonished when she said that the president would speak to him right away, he'd been awaiting his call. In an hour, the police had surrounded the office. But neither the lawyer nor his client were there any longer. The client went away in the same way he'd come, with his hat, overcoat and dark glasses, not without explaining to the lawyer that, from that moment on, they would not see each other again, and he would get all his instructions by phone or mail. The payment, as well. Before he went out, the client left the first instalment, in cash, and the envelope which the lawyer had to take personally to the meeting with the board of the central bank in Paris. When the police arrived, the lawyer was already at home, next to his wife sitting on the sofa with a glass of whisky in her hand. Since the client's first visit, he hadn't told her anything. Neither did he mention the business that night. When she asked him what he was going to do in Paris the next day, he answered: 'Business meeting', and that was that. It was already two months since the game of horrors had begun. The envelope the client had left him was sealed. The next day, as had been agreed, he handed it to the board of directors of the central bank. The president opened the envelope and took out a sheet of paper covered with numbers. The sheet passed from hand to hand around the table – except for the lawyer, of course – and returned to the president. The meeting lasted no more than five minutes. The president turned to the computer technician's lawyer, and said he could inform his client that the council would make its position known in the next few days. Before leaving, the lawyer recounted what had happened on the previous day, when the police surrounded his office. He said he hoped disagreeable incidents like that would not be repeated. The president guaranteed it would not happen again. Some ten days later, and after telling the client in detail about the meeting in Paris, the lawyer got a call from the president of the central bank. The old man demanded the phone number of the computer technician, or his address, anything, anything, he shouted down the phone, while the lawyer tried to explain that, even if he wanted to hand his client over, he couldn't, simply because he had not the least idea of his phone number, much less where he lived, for his client only phoned from public phone boxes, and at the most unexpected times, to prevent the police catching up with him. That was when the president asked for one more piece of proof: 'I want one more piece of proof.' 'Proof of what?' asked the lawyer, revealing his absolute ignorance, which in some sense proved his innocence, acted as his alibi. 'Tell him I want one more piece of proof. He'll understand', replied the president, and hung up. The lawyer understood less and less. And the role of a mere messenger began to irritate him. He wanted to know what he was dealing with. What the secret shared by his client and the country's banking system was. During the next call, he asked the client, who said again what he'd already said when he hired him: that it was better for his own safety for him not to know. 'What I've discovered is huge. What I know could turn the whole financial system upside down.' It was only then that the lawyer became certain that he was an intermediary in a blackmail of nation-wide proportions, involving the country's whole financial system. He realised, without knowing exactly what they were talking about, that the president of the central bank wanted that new piece of evidence as proof of the technician's knowledge of a state secret. 'More than that', the client corrected him over the phone. 'I've discovered something they didn't know. They should thank me. It's taken three years of my life to uncover a secret capable of turning the whole financial system upside down. I don't mean to use it. I'm not threatening anything. I'm not blackmailing anyone. All I want is to be paid for my discovery. Like any inventor or scientist. I'll sell my discovery and the subject will be closed. They buy my discovery and they'll have my silence as a free gift. They should thank me, but they treat me like a criminal.' That was when the lawyer began to glimpse what his wife would express so well in those words, sitting on the sofa, almost three months after the third and last appearance of the client in his office, with a glass of whisky in her hand, 'in the American style': 'For you, the best thing would be if he didn't exist, he's your weak point'. What was she saying? Who was she talking about? How could she know exactly what had been taking over his mind in the last few months? How had she found out? The only time he'd mentioned the client to her was when he came back from the first meeting with the board of the central bank in Paris. He was frightened by it all and couldn't stop himself. It's human. He briefly commented, or, better, let slip a few words about the client and the numbers, the sheet covered with numbers, illegible even for someone who, like her, spent all their time doing accounts. But he said nothing more, because he soon saw the potential of the case and its possible developments, which didn't exclude the elimination of the computer technician, which would be easy in a way, since no one had ever seen him, but only if he was silly enough to reappear. Because all he had to do was put his

foot in his office for the police to swoop. The ideal
thing would be for the lawyer to find out where he
was hiding. But even then he couldn't eliminate him
before he knew his secret. His hands were tied. It
would happen to him, with his mental block with
numbers. Before he eliminated the client, he needed
his secret to go on with the blackmail. It was an
ideal plan. Instead of the honorariums the client had
pledged himself to pay in monthly instalments, he
would get all the money from the blackmail. He had
understood the huge danger of the situation, but
without the least idea of what it was about. He
needed to discover the secret so he could go on nego-
tiating as an intermediary, only now for a dead man,
and then pocket all the money, with the advantage,
on top of that, of coming out of it clean. He didn't
blink when he got the second sealed envelope, in the
mail, a month and a half after the first, the confir-
mation of the proof the president demanded and
that he had to take personally to Paris. He didn't
think twice before he opened it and came upon
another sheet of paper covered with numbers. It was
irritating. Why numbers? And why did it have to be

him, who'd had problems with algebra since he was a child? He looked out a mathematician, with no success. The guy only confirmed the obvious, that there must be some kind of code there, because of the combination, frequency and alternation of the figures, but that you'd have to start from some kind of basic parameter to decipher it. You'd have to know what each number represented, and the place it occupied in the whole, and know the language it was written in and the formula, to be able to read it. The lawyer left in a state of irritation. He was so irritated he didn't even think to put the sheet away when he got home in the middle of the night. He left it open on the table. What danger was there, if it was illegible? He only picked it up again in the morning. He left for Paris earlier than necessary, to consult other mathematicians before the second meeting with the bankers the following day. But he got the same reply. The sheet was illegible without the establishment of a set convention on which to base an interpretation, without some kind of semantics. 'I could have told you that!' shouted the lawyer at one of the mathematicians,

the third he'd seen on the same afternoon in Paris,
a little old man with white hair and a smock, who
immediately threw him out of his room at the
university shouting curses in Russian, his first
language, which he hadn't spoken since childhood,
though it was still his favourite. Nobody had the
least idea of what was written there, but when, at
the meeting, the president of the central bank
opened the envelope, before passing it on to the
board of directors, he slumped into his chair with
his hands on his head, desperately stammering:
'This is the proof'. That sent the lawyer madder
still. If these bankers could read the combination
of numbers, how was it possible no one else could?
He was so upset that, instead of waiting till night
to go back home, on the train, he decided to get the
first plane back in the early afternoon. He couldn't
lose any more time. He had to find the client before
the police did. He had to eliminate him, not without first convincing him of the impossible, to tell
him his secret, he needed to decipher what those
figures said. When they came out of the airport,
which was some thirty miles away from the ruins of

the libertine baron's château, and the hill where
they lived, the wife said they needed to pick up a
package in the town before they went back home.
While she was paying for the package, he went into
the chemist's to buy some tranquillisers which he'd
been increasingly taking in the last few weeks, and,
when he came out, he came face to face with a most
unexpected scene: the client, without dark glasses,
hat or overcoat, talking very animatedly, on the other
side of the street, with his wife, who already had the
package in her hand. Everything went dark and he
very nearly fell down in the middle of the street. It
wasn't just him. The client, too, couldn't have imagined he would come across him there. It's probable
he thought the lawyer was still in Paris, as agreed,
and decided to take advantage of the afternoon to
do what he had to do in the town, thinking he was
in safe territory. Neither could he have imagined that
that was the man's wife. The lawyer crossed the road
and approached his wife. The client went pale. For
a few seconds, the two looked at each other in mysti-
fied silence. The lawyer could see for the first time
the expression of horror, and not the impassive face

the computer technician had appeared with on the three occasions he'd been to the office. He was dressed in jeans, trainers and a white T-shirt. It's difficult to imagine which of the two was the more astonished. But they managed to hide it, because she hardly saw. Luckily, the lawyer had not been followed by the police. The two pretended they didn't know each other when the woman introduced them: 'Monsieur . . . I am sorry! What was your name? This is my husband'. They shook hands. The client, suddenly very nervous, said he needed to leave, he was late, that it was a pleasure to see her again and meet her husband, and disappeared. As soon as he was gone, the lawyer turned round to his wife and asked, his eyes burning, where she knew that man from. She asked him if he remembered the day when, months ago, she had completely lost control of the car and crashed into a tree in the middle of a maize-field. 'Well, that was the man who helped me. I think he lives somewhere around here.' The lawyer still tried to follow him. He ran as far as the corner, but there was no sign of the client. He came back, grabbed the woman by the arms with all his strength and shook her right there in the street, trying to get more information out of her. He insisted on knowing where the accident had taken place. At first, she still laughed, said he was hurting her, that he was mad, and asked where so much jealousy had come from, so suddenly. But she soon saw that her husband was not in a joking mood; he was beside himself. He dragged her to the car and asked again where the accident had happened. He asked her a thousand times, yelling at her, while, shaking, she tried to remember where the maize-field was. He carried on shouting as he drove along the road, asking what else she was hiding, why she'd never said she knew that man. He left her in the house and went out in the car, at a furious speed, following her instructions. He was determined to discover where the client lived before nightfall. He only came back after dark. That was when she, sitting on the sofa with a glass of whisky in her hand, greeted him with those fateful words, mocking what seemed to her an unexpected attack of jealousy: 'For you, the best thing would be if he didn't exist, he's your weak point'. She might have been talking about

anyone they'd met in the street, and not specifically
about the client, for she didn't even know who he
was. She might have talking about God. Or about
the baron and his philosophy of treachery. But that
wasn't the way he understood it. His weakness was
numbers. She must be talking about something else.
She must know about something. But now he finally
had a clue as to the whereabouts of the client, who
only rang from telephones the police couldn't track
down, from public phone boxes, from a different
place each time, from the most diverse areas of the
country, hundreds of miles apart from each other,
just like the post offices from which he posted his
envelopes, without the least logic to them – now he
finally had a clue he couldn't miss the opportunity.
For months, he'd tried to find the client. He was
excited, as if he'd finally uncovered a bit of the
secret, and violated his intimacy. But it was just an
illusion. More than ever, he had to be careful he
wasn't being followed, hand the client over to the
police and the bankers without meaning to, so to
speak, now he had gone half way. All the way home,
he didn't stop thinking for a moment. He had to get

rid of the client before the police or the bankers found him, but he couldn't kill him without knowing his secret. He couldn't open himself to the possibility of the bankers asking for a new piece of proof and having nothing to show them. He needed to discover the secret at all costs before he killed the client. It was probable that all this had been thought through from the beginning by the computer technician himself, who could trust no one. He wasn't going to put his life in the hands of a provincial lawyer without some kind of guarantee. His trump card was his secret. It was the guarantee that the lawyer wouldn't kill him. 'You will be tempted by contra-dictory desires.' Nobody could continue the black-mail without him, without knowing the secret. Because the secret was him, in person. Without him, the secret would disappear. The plan the lawyer drew up, on his way back home, was anything but perfect, but, in the circumstances, it was the best he could have found. He would ask the client for a new series of proofs, and would make out that it was the bankers' demand. And, instead of sending them to Paris, he would keep them for any eventuality, after he'd got rid of the client. He would keep a stock of proofs for when he needed them, even though he hadn't the least idea of what they meant. The plan was anything but perfect, but there was no other option. Now he had a clue as to where the client lived (there weren't many houses in that area, near the maize-field), he had to hurry before he himself disappeared, for he was no fool, and of course he must be expecting the worst possible outcome after the unexpected encounter in the town. He got home with the whole plan in his head, and was received by his wife sitting on the sofa, with a glass of whisky in her hand: 'For you, the best thing would be if he didn't exist, he's your weak point'. Who did she mean, he? How could she have come out with that? But he couldn't ask. With those words, she signed her own death warrant, as they say in gangster movies. The next week, while he was planning the client's death, the lawyer planned hers too. He didn't know what she was talking about, but he couldn't risk losing everything because of a simple doubt. He discovered where the client lived and hired his wife's killers. It was the time for her to take steps too, while the

husband was making his international calls. She got
suspicious. She put two and two together. She did
her accounts and sketched out her revenge, while
he was agreeing that they would shoot him in the
leg. Everything to make it look convincing. It was
the price to pay. The lawyer observed the client's
house more than once, from a distance, without being
seen. On the day before the journey, she read to her
husband, in bed, a chapter from the collected works
of the baron. The part where the author explained
vengeance as pleasure. She read sitting on his belly,
leaning against his thighs. It was months since they'd
slept together. The fact is that he felt his desire
rekindled, excited that he was going to kill her in
two days' time, that this would be the last time:
'You will be tempted by contradictory desires'. He
was invaded by the morbid thrill of thinking that
this body which was giving in to him would be dead
in less than two days. That was why he hardly heard
what she was reading aloud: 'You who are still young
and beautiful – and precisely because you are – have,
amongst all of us, the greatest chance of breaking
through the bars of the human prison in horror and

in revenge. Just because they are young and beautiful, those who could get the greatest benefit from
horror and revenge don't take advantage of this
potential while they still can, they are tricked first
by their families and the Church, and then by their
marriage, only to discover when they have been
disarmed by years of dedication, reproduction and
submission to the same logic which subjects us all,
that they have missed the chance to free the human
being from the prison in which he has locked himself,
in the dark, unable to see further than his own nose,
ignorant of his own condition, uselessly trying to
contain his own instincts. I exhort you, my love, to
make of me an instrument of your revenge and
horror, my most sincere vocation, which can only
be achieved through the hands of a beautiful young
girl like you. I exhort you, my deflowered damsel,
to make of your lost maidenhood an implacable arm
against the logical illogicality of conventions which
prevent us from revealing ourselves in all our natu-
ral splendour. Make this world in which we lived
confined, as in a dark cell, as unbearable and incomprehensible for them as it already is for us'. She was

reading aloud while he was getting a hard-on and coming, as if he were deaf, though nowadays he repeats the same passage, by heart, over and over. That baron is a terrible writer. At the time he didn't see that that book had become her manual, her bible, that she'd learned the lesson, and was ready to put those teachings into practice. She made no real objections to the journey, after asking with that 'American style' smile if it wasn't a very dangerous city. And she got the most barefaced guarantee: that nothing can abolish chance, that if it didn't happen here, it would be in Bangkok or the Yemen or Istanbul or some other place. And she agreed, not knowing yet that he was talking about her death. She had to disappear, the moment she said those words, her eyes shining and a glass of whisky in her hand. She preferred not to realise that at bottom he was referring to her death, but subconsciously she already knew or guessed, because she wouldn't have set up the theatrical reversal of fortunes if she hadn't known. Everything was completely synchronised so he would only realise he'd lost at the last minute, when the collapse and the disappointment of the discovery would be too great for him, making him unable to bear the rest of his life. She calculated her revenge with an inhuman precision. She staged a horror capable of dragging along with it the logic of the dark cell they were confined in and, making him finally see, made the world so incomprehensible and unbearable to him, and as dark as hers would be when she was dead. Her revenge was to make the blind man see in the dark and the deaf man hear in the silence. He fell in the undergrowth with a leg-wound. His wife's face was buried in the earth. She had flown forwards, cutting through the brushwood, to end up face-down in the earth, dead. Checkmate. He tried to pull himself together. He had to find someone who would take him to the police. In the station, he said they'd been victims of a robbery. He said they'd gone in the car of a man who'd approached them in the airport. They saw nothing unusual in that. They thought everything was fine until they saw they were going out of the city, pass-ing by shacks, heaps of rubbish, vacant lots. That was when she'd objected and been slapped on the face for the first time. They took an unmade road in an area of wasteland; yes, he would recognise it, he could take them there. They stopped the car and after taking everything from them, money, jewellery, credit cards, they made the two of them get out and run, and while they were running he heard two shots and saw his wife fall, and then another shot and he felt an awful pain in his leg and flung himself on the ground, desperate, beside her, as if he were dead, dead like her, so they would go away, and leave him beside his only reason for living, the wife who had been with him at every moment, in all the worst crises of his life, even in the midst of horrors, and had never abandoned him; he lay beside her in the hope of being able to save her also. And when he was certain they'd gone away, he left walking as best he could, because all he could think of was how to save her, of finding someone to save her, bringing her back from death. That was how he told the story to the police. What had they come here for? To have a good time. They were on holiday. They wanted to enjoy the happiness of their marriage in peace, like in a dream. They couldn't have expected that. It wasn't right, it wasn't right. The policemen took them back to the scene of the crime, guided by the unfortunate soul who'd found him lost in the middle of the piles of rubbish and the open sewers, limping along an unmade road. 'The world stinks'. That was what the officer said to the interpreter they'd sent from the consulate. But no one said anything, while they were passing through the mud and the huts till they got the body of the Frenchwoman covered in flies. 'It wasn't exactly the way you thought your journey would end, right?', the officer asked and the interpreter translated. But no one replied anything. They took him to a hospital to attend to his leg. He asked to be able to go back home. He said he would continue to collaborate in any way necessary to catch those responsible. 'No one is responsible in this stinking world', said the officer to the interpreter, who didn't translate. 'This is really bad for the image of the city. Really bad.' Three days later, they took him to the airport. The interpreter and the policeman accompanied him. He said he wanted to buy French newspapers. He went into the shop on his own, while the interpreter and the policeman waited for him outside, and when he came out he'd already lost his head. He turned round to the policeman and said he insisted on being called baron, a demand the interpreter translated without realising the Frenchman had gone mad. The foreign newspapers always came late. He'd bought a French paper of three days ago, of the day they'd got here, he and his wife, the day when she was murdered. He came out of the newspaper shop with the copy of the paper folded in his hand; on the front page was the news of the arrest of the computer technician: 'Plan to destroy the country's financial system uncovered and aborted'. The client had been arrested on the same night they boarded the plane. While they were boarding, he had been detained by forty armed police, who surrounded his house, twenty miles from Lagrange, in the south of France. Now he'd been arrested, no one would ever know the secret. He read the news when he was still in the shop, and when he came out he'd already lost his head. He'd had his wife killed for no reason. She worked it all out. She must have seen the sheet covered in numbers on the table. She was always doing sums. She was a wizard at numbers. She worked it all out. Just at the right moment. She'd sent a letter to the bankers. She revealed the computer technician's whereabouts. And, while they were boarding, he had been arrested twenty miles from the baron's château. The Frenchman was gripped by the horror she'd left him as an inheritance in the airport newspaper shop, with a three-day old paper in his hand. A horror cap-able of sweeping away all the logic of this stinking world, where no one is responsible for anything. We are all victims of the horror, even when we're killing, we are innocent victims of the horror, we are what we are so as to prove God doesn't exist, said the Frenchman to the policeman, when he came out of the newspaper shop, and that was when the interpreter realised there was no point in translating, for he was no longer making any sense. Horror is the only thing that doesn't die. There's no consolation for horror. They didn't believe he had really ordered his wife's murder. But neither could they let him go after the confession. They didn't find the killers. They had no proof. They needed proof. Yet another robbery with murder. And the man had gone mad. They didn't know what to

do with him. He became violent. He couldn't travel.
He no longer knew where he was going. They
interned him here, just in case, while they awaited
proof. The family in France haven't said anything.
They didn't want to know. The case was insoluble.
The police didn't want to let him leave. Because of
the confession. Despite the story he's been repeating for years, and that I've just told you, there's
nothing to prove he had his wife killed. The obvious doesn't provide proof, though the world needs
it. However much he insists, no one believes him.
Officially, it was a robbery. No one thinks he's not
mad. And that's what he repeats over and over again.
That he killed his wife and that he's not mad. I'm
tired of hearing the same story. Every crisis he has,
it's the same litany. I know it all by heart. Sometimes
he gets violent. The rest of his life waiting for proof,
to prove God doesn't exist. He came here saying he
was the baron of whatever looking for the Marquis
de Sade. Every now and then, as if he were confessing, he tells the story over again, in detail. This only
lasts the time it takes to tell the whole story and
then he says again that he's baron so-and-so, and he's

looking for the Marquis de Sade. He thinks he's in
a French asylum at the beginning of the nineteenth
century and that only the marquis can save him.
Then another crisis comes on and he begins to howl
that he wants out of here. He's afraid. He has hallucinations. He sees things. He talks to himself as if
he were hearing voices. He thinks he's not alone. He
hears voices and talks to them. We move him to
another room and two days later he has the same
hallucinations. He shouts for the light to be switched
on in broad daylight; he's afraid of being alone
because he says there's someone else there: 'You will
be tempted by contradictory desires'. And on top
of that he's a racist. The last time I tried to calm
him down, he thought I was the devil. Because I'm
black. He can't stand the sight of me. Go on then,
you go in, and when he yells at you that he's a dead
man, that he's seen the devil in person, that we're
all dead, try to explain to him that this is not hell
and he's not dead, but tactfully, go on, try and
convince the guy we're in Rio de Janeiro.

ON THE WRITER /
CHARACTER

Donatien Alphonse François, the Marquis de Sade, was born in 1740 in Paris, and died in 1814, in the Charenton lunatic asylum, where he had been interned since 1803 and where he used to put on plays with the inmates. The inescapably radical views expressed in his literary work and his libertine philosophy led to him spending a good part of his life in prison. His biography is punctuated by sexual scandals, escapes and imprisonments. He married against his will in 1763. Five years later, accused of forcing the prostitute Rose Keller to physical punishment on the pretext of testing a new healing ointment, he spent more than seven months in jail. In 1772, after an orgy with his servant and four women in Marseilles, he was accused of poisoning, fled to Italy, and was condemned to death

FEAR OF DE SADE

'for contumacy'. He was finally caught near the Swiss border, though he was to escape with his wife's help. He was arrested again in 1777 and transferred to the Bastille in 1784, where he wrote some of his masterpieces, such as *One Hundred and Twenty Days of Sodom*. These manuscripts were stolen during the taking of the Bastille in 1789. Again at liberty, for a short time he collaborated with the French Revolution as an ordinary citizen, but the radical singularity of his views was incompatible with the new political and social order, and the marquis was finally condemned to death for 'moderatism'. He was saved by the death of Robespierre. His château, at Lacoste in the south of France, was sold. He lived in poverty until he was arrested again in 1801, accused of writing pornography by the counter-revolutionaries, who saw his texts as literary manifestos for the Terror. Titles such as *The Philosopher in the Bedroom*, *Aline and Valcour*, *Justine* or *Juliette*, among others, caused indignation and were banned for almost two hundred years after they were written. In 1957, the publisher Jean-Jacques Pauvert was prosecuted in France for publishing Sade's books. The stir provoked by his strange work is due in part to the libertine scenes which he describes – in which men and women are like mechanical parts of a great sexual machine – but above all to his implacable philosophical views, which expose the paradox of the human condition, its tragic foundations and the hypocrisy of moral and social codes. In 1801, a contemporary wrote about Sade:

If the pleasure that the exercise of virtue gives me is of the same nature as physical enjoyment, [. . .] if the approval of my conscience is nothing more than an agreeable tickling of my nerves, how could I reply to the person who prefers one pleasure to another? What can I say to the criminal or the assassin who gets pleasure from his crimes, unless it is that he should take care he doesn't get punished for them?

B.C.

ON THE AUTHOR

Bernardo Carvalho was born in 1960 in Rio de Janeiro. He is a writer, journalist, and weekly columnist for the *Folha de São Paulo*. As well as *Fear of de Sade*, he has published a collection of stories, *Aberração* [Aberration] and the novels *Onze* [Eleven], *Os bêbados e os sonâmbulos* [Drunks and Sleepwalkers], *Teatro* [Drama], *As iniciais* [The Initials], *Nove noites* [Nine nights] and *Mongólia*. Some of these books have also been published in France, Portugal, Italy and Sweden.